THE HAUNTED WOODS

NICHOLAS LEWIS

PublishAmerica
Baltimore

Hardcover 978-1-4560-2760-5
Softcover 978-1-4560-2761-2
PUBLISHED BY PUBLISHAMERICA, LLLP
www.publishamerica.com
Baltimore

Printed in the United States of America

Dedicated to the children who lost their childhood in the dark recess behind the light.

The Haunted Woods

Once upon a time, there was a place where people chose to be victimized...where people chose to be scared as a thrill, all in the name of good Halloween fun.

Children saw it as a right of passage, a growing up experience.
Adults saw it as a way to place fear in the mind of the adolescent.

They saw it as open season...

***

"There has got to be something really wrong here! They're in the parade, chasing little kids with chainsaws. People are running and screaming through the woods, falling and hurting themselves because they can't see due to it being pitch black or the strobe lights in their face! We were stupid. We accepted this as normal. It was only a matter of time..."

"A matter of time for what?!"

"For the killing to stop being make-believe. It was never in good fun."

Contents

Prologue

Tractor trailers zoom up and down Goodman Highway. In the small farm communities that are connected by its path, children are getting ready for the fall festivities: hay rides, carnivals, parades, trick or treating, and ultimately going to *The Haunted Woods.*

After Halloween, there isn't much to look forward to other than Thanksgiving and Christmas break. Everyone seems to make the most out of the last bit of warm weather before settling into a long winter of dreaded snow and sleet—everyone including the Jaycee's. *The Haunted Woods,* a legend all in its own, but a nightmare to those that lived through it, was their time to really shine. People would come from all over the "heartland" for one night of Hell.

Waterville, Missouri never had that great of a reputation to begin with, but this situation always manages to get brought up. I can't tell people that I'm from there without them asking me about it. I usually lie, say I moved around a lot, and tell people that it was just a myth. If they're not from there, they don't know and for the most part, the younger generation doesn't know much about it; either because they were toddlers or they weren't even born yet. It's been so long ago. It only seemed appropriate that someone would try to rehash everything and start the bullshit all over again. People are idiots.

It's been years since the Jaycee's put on this public display of monstrosity. The last year was enough for the county to deal with. Everything was hushed up rather quickly. Rumors even surfaced that the local Jaycees disbanded in order to smooth things over. The disappearances and then when it became a feeding frenzy—no one could have stopped it from happening, but they broke up anyway. It made a lot of people wonder if it had somehow been planned all along. They knew it could happen and year after year, from 1982 to 1987, it spread until there were other towns outside of the county involved in the tradition. The other towns set up their own form of *The Haunted Woods*. Yet, it all came back to the beginning, to the woods on the highway outside of town.

For a couple years, it was moved to the Lafayette's woods on the other side of Waterville. On one side of the highway was a big farm house with the woods behind it. Across the highway was a massive pond with the interstate on the other side of it. It was too obvious that this location was too much of a liability. Surprisingly, it wasn't this that posed a threat. The farmer couldn't handle the crowds of people every night. The noise and vandalism got to be too much, so he put a stop to it and *The Haunted Woods* went back to their natural habitat; a breeding ground for malevolence.

It seemed only natural for *The Haunted Woods* to be in its first place of origin. Otherwise, it just wasn't as scary. I can tell you first hand that there was something about those set of woods that will haunt me until the day I die. I can't drive past them on the way to the town I was raised in without staring and wondering if something or someone is going to come out of those woods bearing an axe or a machete. It's surreal and just damn creepy.

The nightmares of what happened eventually faded, as does everything. Seeing a shrink, anti-anxiety pills, staying busy all the time, and as far the fuck away from that county as possible has helped. Oh, every once in a while I have a good one, but usually it's so random that it doesn't even make sense why I'm having the nightmare or what it's actually about, there's just this overall sense of fear.

For the most part, I became a shut-in. I wouldn't say that I necessarily have agoraphobia; it's more of a recluse sort of situation. I prefer to stay at home. It's been a good while since I had a panic attack. It's slowly but surely getting better. I mainly have a problem going to places I've never been or meeting new people for fear of what might happen. It gets hard to trust even those that I am familiar with, much less a stranger. So, I stay at home, watch movies, cook, and play games on the internet, whatever…it works for me.

In college, I was heavily medicated. And I drank a lot, which probably didn't help but it made me black out so I could sleep. I eventually got a job waiting tables. Bad idea at first, but it gave me money. I had to take pills before I left the house, and usually one before I got out of the car to go inside the restaurant. As with most corporate chains, a family environment is the atmosphere that they try to go for. And as well with any restaurant, the cooks smoke a lot of weed. So, sometimes during the shift, I would go out back and take a drag or two off a one-hitter. It usually did the trick better than smoking a cigarette. Then, I would go back to doing whatever it was that I was doing before.

Now, here I am, forty, single, living in a country home outside of St. Genevieve, Mo. But to get to this point, we have to go back to the beginning. We have to start the nightmare that was my life all over. And I can't do that without going back to the town I was raised in...back to high school. Maybe some clarification will come out of it or maybe it will make things worse. Who knows?

***

Halloween, 1987. The last year of *The Haunted Woods.*

I guess I should introduce myself while I have you here. My name is Kyle Nathaniel Harper. I have this recurring dream that I'm standing at the bottom of a hill unable to see on the other side and then this massive tidal wave comes over the top of the hill consuming everything in its path.

I stand there frozen, watching as I'm swept away, drowning in the strong current of this cold blue water. Sometimes I'm attacked by "Jaws," but most of the time I just drown. Then, I wake up short of breath but relieved that it was only a dream.

I know it sounds odd, but it's a dream that I've had ever since I can remember. For me, life in 1987 is nearly perfect. I'm the captain of the varsity basketball team; I'm dating a beautiful little Brit foreign exchange student, named Melanie Hopkins. She's smart as a whip and I'm just blown away by how much she knows and how much she has read. It's pretty obvious that she's going to be our Valedictorian. How she ended up in our little po-dunk town, I have no clue, but she's a cool chick.

I have a new Chevy. I didn't get to pick out the color though,

I didn't want a white one, but that's what I got. Oh well, beggars can't be choosy, right? I could still be walking instead of driving. The funny thing is that I'm so used to walking everywhere that I still don't drive that much. I have a new truck and it mostly sits in the driveway.

One problem that I do have is that my dad is gone. He's been gone since I was little. Town gossip is that my mother cheated on him and he caught her—with a guy from our church no less. Needless to say, she got custody as most women do, and he flew the coop. He remarried and disappeared, I haven't seen him since. Maybe it's for the best.

Mom is like tainted goods now. Oh, every once in a while, we'll have a gentleman caller, but she tries her best to be discreet. Maybe she should have thought of that the first time. But even with the secret affairs she has had the past few years, still no ring. I almost feel bad for her, but she brought this on herself. I have to keep telling myself that. Every time I start to hate my dad for not being around, I have to remind myself that it's not his fault. She did this to him. She did this to our family. She's the reason why my dad is no longer around. Then, I get pissed at her instead. Eventually, I just go for a walk and try to think about something else. A person can only stay in one mood for so long before it becomes tiresome. And I don't want to hate my mother. I don't hate my mother, I'm just not sure if I love her or not.

I like to wait until the last possible minute before I get out of bed in the morning and the last possible minute that I have to arrive to class before being counted as tardy. Sleep time is very valuable or anytime that's not school time. My grades have slacked off since freshman year, but hey, what kid doesn't need a break? The only problem was that I have been on a break for the past two years, long enough for the Go-go's to break up and get back together, long enough for my friend's parents to split up and get back together, but not long enough for me to get my act together. I keep busy, but I'm not necessarily the over-achiever type. My grades just don't seem all that important anymore. My dad used to always harp on good grades in elementary, a strong work ethic, tidiness, and promptness—and look at where it got him. These days, I basically have the theory that if you are absent from your own life, then how in the hell can you expect others to show up? My dad was always doing the "right thing," yet he never did the right thing. Sometimes you have to take care of home first and he never really did that.

I guess you could say that I've become self-involved. I enjoy being at the mercy of the crowd. It's nice having that approval which I never got from my parents. Sure, I got stuff because I'm their only child. It's just that most of the time, I feel like I'm more of a pet than a child. She buys my affection. She pats me on the head. She should have bought a Schnauzer.

I have a typical morning ritual. I lay in bed staring at the wall or out the window for five minutes after my alarm clock goes off or mom wakes me up. To me, there's no need to rush out of bed. It can't be good for your heart to hit the ground running when you first wake up. Dad used to always say, "I want to see your feet hit the floor." I'd sit up, turn, place my feet on the ground and mock stretch, he'd leave, and I'd lie back down. To hell with that, this isn't a military household. I'm not one of the troops in basic training. It's just school or it's just church, it ain't nothing important. I mean it's not like I'm in a prep school or some other private school where academic distinction is a priority. I go to a small town public school where the only thing that matters is football games and basketball homecoming. The rest is just filler.

After I lay there and finish waking up, I use the *lou* (that's my new favorite word Melanie taught me), then I wash my face. A lot of times I don't shower in the morning because I shower and shave my little mustache before I go to bed. Plus, it allows for me to sleep an extra ten to fifteen minutes; like I said, sleep is key. I get dressed, douse myself with Ralph Lauren or Calvin Klein cologne, and then I'm out the door. Most of the time, I don't eat breakfast in the morning. For some odd reason, it tears my stomach up. I can't even have a soda, coffee, or orange juice in the morning or otherwise I'm cramping within thirty minutes to an hour. I don't know how I began to have such a nervous stomach. Any other time, I'm fine. Well, except for the bladder issue.

I swear, I have the world's smallest bladder. I pee constantly, especially when I get nervous. I have to pee three or four times before I go on the court for a game. I completely quit drinking any liquid for an hour or so before each game so I don't have an issue. When we're in mid, the first place I head to in the locker room is the lou. I'm just afraid that one of these times I'm going to be pissing and get stuck when I need to be elsewhere. It does get annoying. My parents used to complain all the time when I was little because I would always get up during church to go pee. I couldn't help it, but since I was disrupting, it was like I was misbehaving. Excuse the hell out of me okay. I would much rather be in a comfortable daze like everyone else, it's just the way things are.

I guess the main reason why my parents were so *annoyed* by my bladder issue was that it was hard to break me from peeing the bed at night when I was little. I used to have nightmares and night terrors. I used to imagine people outside my window, people standing in my doorway. Well, men, these were never women. I was never scared of a woman. For some reason the only dreams I had about females were sexual, even at five or six years old. No, it was always a scary older man outside my window or standing in my doorway. Thinking about it now, maybe I was projecting my insecurities about my overbearing father and I was physically manifesting something that wasn't there before—could be.

Needless to say, I would get my ass beat every morning I woke up and the bed was wet. I never had to make my bed until I was almost ten or eleven. Granted, I had stopped peeing the bed by the time I was in first grade, but I guess my mother was in the habit of checking every morning. They thought I was just a bad seed. Who knows what they think now?

So, after I get on my way and finally leave the house, I usually stop by and pick up any random stragglers that want a ride or I stop by and pick up Melanie. It's funny, after I got this truck, I became everyone's taxi cab and new best friend. I don't mind it though. It's nice to have people that want to be around you, it keeps you from feeling lonely. At first, there were a lot of people jealous and there were a few comments made about me being a spoiled brat and "daddy pays for everything." I can't help it if I am more fortunate than others. I'm very grateful for what I have. My parents decided to educate themselves and get high-paying jobs. It's not our fault if the other people in this town didn't do the same. Don't blame me for you not having anything, blame your parents for not providing as they should. My dad's absentee, but he still picks up the tab, which is a hell of a lot more than I can say for most of my friends' dads.

I usually don't start getting hounded for rides by these jealous people until it gets too cold to walk. Luckily for me, it's the fourth week of October and it's still mildly pleasant outside. Although I wouldn't necessarily call it shorts weather, it's still mid 60's. As soon as people start wearing sweaters and jackets, that's when they come a-running.

I used to do the same thing once I thought I was too old to ride the bus to school. Granted, this meant I had to walk for two years until I turned sixteen, but I wasn't riding with the kiddies. I guess I swapped one headache for the other. I never really liked the people that rode my bus. They were always running their mouths; calling me names…I actually had one kid call me a nerd and asked me if I was a straight-A student. It was stupid. We had a ton of kids on our route that wouldn't ride the bus because some idiot in the back was always saying stupid shit. Eventually, you just got tired of arguing and ignoring never worked, if anything, it just seemed to make it worse because they would keep going until you paid attention to them. I've never like bullies. If anything I've always wanted extremely bad shit to happen to them. You know, other than the fact that their home-life is royally fucked up which made them this way. I'm talking about physical and psychological pain. There's nothing more cathartic than watching a kid that hurts other children get their nose broken, break their arm, or end up paralyzed from an accidental fall or car crash. Karma's a bitch.

We actually had one bully that died freshman year. His name was Abner, which made him seem completely comical and what possibly made him so hateful since he was teased about it growing up by everyone and their brother. He was a senior and dickhead. Well, dickhead decided one night while drinking with some of the other assholes that he could swing from one tree to the next like a drunkin' monkey. Needless to say, he didn't make it. Nobody cared either except the assholes he was with. It just goes to show you that being a complete dick to everyone will only serve to push them away and make them hate you.

What's really comical about that story is that his fellow assholes left him out there. One of the little tramps from our grade was out there as well. When she came home, she started crying and told her mumsy and her mom called the cops. See, even his own people deserted him in death. That's proof that you can't treat everybody like shit all the time or anytime for that matter.

Of course, we all had to pretend like it was this great tragedy to our school. *We lost one of our own. What ever will we do?* Um, I don't know, be grateful for one less asshole on this earth. He was destined for the factory. He had no motivation to play sports, join clubs, make anything remotely close to a "C" average, and his people skills sucked. What else could he do besides menial labor? Well, unless he wanted to go into politics...but that would require that he would have to dress up and possibly join something, so not likely.

For me, I just looked at the situation as a stepping stone; if only we could get rid of the rest of the slacker bunch. Sure, sometimes they would say stupid stuff that would make you giggle, but most of the time you just disregarded them. They were definitely not people to be counted on for anything, and they had no concept of pressure. They just liked being all aloof and making fun of every damn thing. If they ever had to try for anything, I'd be shocked.

Along with everyone else, I always would see them walking to school. Well, when they weren't terrorizing people on the bus. I will have to admit that there were times when I wanted to swerve and knock their ass into the ditch. I remember what it was like being a freshman and being picked on by the junior and senior slackers. The guys on my basketball team never fucked with me, nor did any of the guys that were in any of the clubs I was in. It's just bizarre to me, that people that don't do shit always have something to say.

Well, two or three would-be victims later and me and whoever are pulling into the school parking lot. We've all gotten kinda hip to showing up when the last bell rings. I figure that we're here long enough during the day, five days a week, and if we do extra-curricular activities, we're here more than that. I think they suck up enough of our time and spirit. *I really can't wait to get out,* is what I'm thinking as I dredge up the sidewalk into the building.

I never know what to expect when I walk onto campus. Every morning it's something different. A fist-fight sometimes brakes out before I arrive and then I have to hear about it until third period, which by then the story has been completely blown out of proportion.

This place always seems so loud and chaotic in the morning. I don't understand it. I'm tired as shit and the last thing I want to be is up this damn early, much less be all shiny and wired. It's like what the hell did these people do; smoke a pound of crack with their coffee in the morning? *Shut up!*

Fortunately for me, my first class is a free period. I'm a TA for Coach Bradfield. And since he doesn't have class until second period, he always shows up late. We basically just talk about the last game, the next game, players and strategy, districts, and then I do some copy work or grade some of his papers. It's easy. For the most part, my whole schedule is pretty easy. I took all the hard classes immediately, that way I could get a bad case of senioritis if I wanted to. It's kind of smart when you think about it. Do everything you can to ensure a victory, then sit back and relax, enjoy the benefits of your hard work.

My schedule looks like this: TA first period, Nutrition second, Senior English third, Weight Training fourth, lunch, Home-ec fifth, Spanish 2 (which I've already taken) sixth, and Chamber Choir last. I have like, no homework. It's fucking awesome. But it still seems like I'm doing a lot. Don't get me wrong. I am smart, and I do have above a three point and I did take AP courses until junior year. I just do less and less each year when it comes to class and more and more outside. I'm diversifying. I'm multi-tasking. I'm padding my resume. I'm well-rounded. I'm the All-American boy. I'm exactly what every college wants. Now, deciding what I want and where I want to go is another issue.

I kinda don't want to play basketball in college. I mean, sure, I'm gonna try out for the team. I'm sure there will be a scholarship in it somewhere for me. I mean I am Varsity Captain. College just seems to be about other stuff. Sports seem to be all you have for excitement in high school. In College, I can stay out all night, rush a fraternity, get a decent-paying job (that I want), get an apartment, go on road trips to places I've never been…basically just everything that this small town doesn't offer. I don't want basketball to get in the way of all that. Plus, I can't afford to screw up my grades at the beginning. I'd like to just be a student only for a while. If I decide to do other stuff, then so be it.

I also don't know where Melanie will end up. We haven't talked all that much about it. She might go back to England. Who knows, she might end up going to Oxford or Cambridge. It would be cool if she stayed here and we could go to college together. Maybe if she decides that she wants to go to college here, we can. At this point, I'm basically just trying to stay a-float and see what happens. I'm open to possibilities…I think.

Chapter 1
(Monday Morning)

Kyle walked down the hall and stopped at his locker. Most of the hall traffic had thinned out. There were usually a few seniors and juniors who hung out at their locker and waited for the last bell before they went to class. Kyle thought he would have run into Melanie before she went to class...but no such luck. Her host mother must have dropped her off early. Sometimes Melanie's host parents weren't too keen on Kyle and Melanie spending that much alone time together; even if they were on their way to school, they were still alone in a vehicle. "Things could happen."

Kyle decided to grab some homework he hadn't done yet out of his locker and head to Coach Bradfield's office. There were two ways to get to the coaches' office behind the gym. One was through the outside walk, which sucked when it was cold. And the other was through the gym, which Kyle preferred, especially because of first period girls' P.E. There were a few girls that wore way-too-tight shirts and short shorts. They were always bending over and stretching and jogging. Kyle liked it when they jumped up and down. And even though they pretended like they were offended, each day it was the same routine. The girls would pretend to catch him watching, "Uh, Kyle!", then they would giggle. Kyle would just grin to himself and keep walking to the coaches' office.

Coach Bradfield was always late so Kyle never had to worry about being tardy. Kyle thought it must be nice to someday have a job where he could show up whenever he wanted. The coaches usually left early too. During seventh period, they would let the kids sneak out the back doors or let them "go to their locker" and never come back. It was cool. It was nice to get a break from the monotony that was high school every once in a while. Some teachers just take their jobs too seriously; they become a stickler for the rules and basically make themselves prudish and miserable. Kyle never understood why some teachers teach. *They don't like kids. They pretty much hate their jobs. No one learns anything from them or thinks of them as their favorite teacher. Why did they become a teacher? Why didn't they get a different job?* Valid questions.

Coach Bradfield was different. He loved his job, when he was there, which might be the reason why he liked his job so much. No one was on his ass to perform or be anywhere on time. He had a family and a life outside of teaching, outside of coaching. His family kind of fell apart though when he and his wife split up. He still had the kids most of the time. They were in elementary school and since he worked at the high school, it was just easier for him to be there with them than it was for their mother. She didn't work in town. She worked in some office a half hour away. Apparently, they just didn't get along anymore and that's why they split up. The whole "high school sweethearts" thing that lasted too long but not long enough scenario. He and Kyle never talked about it, even though Coach

Bradfield knew that Kyle's parents weren't together just like he and his wife weren't. It seemed to be too personal to talk about to one of his students and Kyle felt the same way.

As usual, the door to the coaches' office would be locked until Coach Bradfield got there, so Kyle would mope around the locker room, grab a Mountain Dew from the soda machine and just wait. Sometimes he would sneak a smoke behind the dumpster outside of the locker room. The coaches knew he smoked, but he never was openly defiant with it and he never brought other students out there...it was like a secret that everyone knew, but no one cared. And it wasn't like an everyday thing, Kyle was careful to not let anyone see him. He did have a reputation to uphold as a well-off, well-to-do, Christian athlete. No need to let the public see any humanity, it would just confuse them.

Kyle almost got caught once on a band trip to one of the semi-final football games. The pep club bus was crowded and Melanie was in band, so guess which bus Kyle ended up on. Which the band director didn't mind, everyone was going and as long as he had a permission slip from his parent, it was fine.

Well, Kyle was friends with Jeremy Black and Eric Wilson, neither of which were that great of an influence, and when Kyle got around them, he played just as much of the part of an antagonist as they did. They fed off of each other. It was almost like a competition to see who could out-do each other. Kyle was competitive already with sports and his grades; it was like he was born with a chip on his shoulder. He had a tough problem with losing anything, even something as petty as this little rivalry.

So the plan was to sneak cigarettes, cigars, dipping tobacco, and alcohol on the bus and someone would have to bring sodas to mix the alcohol with. Well no one wanted to play the bitch, so they all brought their own stash. What they did was hide it in their pillows, which everyone on the bus brought pillows or a cover, so nobody thought anything about it. Kyle was smart and he knew that they would be checking bags or pockets, so anything that wouldn't be too uncomfortable went in the waistband of his underwear. Everything seemed foolproof, until...

Kyle and Jeremy were juniors. Eric was a freshman. They had been smoking and drinking a little longer than he had and had been around the high school faculty a little bit longer as well...

Unfortunately, Eric got fucked up on the way up to the game, needless to say. And as with most people when they drink, his bravado started to kick in. He got a little loud, a little aggressive, and pretty much made an ass out of himself. His little girlfriend broke up with him in the midst of all of this, which could have and did make the situation that much worse. Well, after he said a few choice words to her and some of the other people in the band, she ratted them all out. What she didn't know was what exactly was going on, all she knew was that her seemingly nice boyfriend was three sheets to the wind and it had something to do with Kyle and Jeremy.

The band director and the bus driver, who was Kyle's preacher, and the new preacher's wife thought they would be slick and let everything die down, ya know, catch everyone off guard. Well, on the way home after the game—which the team had lost, and it was freezing cold watching the game too which made it suck twice as much—they decided to stop at this town and let everyone go grab something to eat at one of the four fast food places that were on the block. Nobody thought anything. Jeremy started getting paranoid and decided that everyone should toss all their stash because he suspected they would go through everyone's stuff when they got off the bus, which they did. They didn't find anything though.

Jeremy, Kyle, and Eric avidly looked for a trash can to pitch the stuff. There was one. It was close, but it was out in the open. It wasn't going to work. The boys walked by it and Jeremy hit the open latch with his fist, which made Kyle and Eric jump. "That's too easy. They'll find it if they look."

"Dude, they're not going to start going through trash cans out here," Kyle said. But he was wrong. Half-way down the block, they looked back and saw Pastor Jim jog over to the trash can and lift the lid to see if they had thrown anything in it. "Well, I'll be damned."

"See, I told you." Jeremy walked a little faster.

"Oh my freakin' God dude, that was close!" Eric looked pale; it was probably because he was already hung over or possibly still drunk.

The boys walked down to the Burger King and thought about throwing the stuff in the restaurant's dumpster, but were majorly paranoid now because they were being watched and the preacher and the band director were checking the trash cans. It just so happened that there was a bar and grill on the other side of the fence that separated the two lots, and their dumpster was wide open right behind the fence. Well, guess where everything went? Well, mostly…

Kyle decided that he would hang on to his Black and Milds. He pulled the pack to the side of his waistband that way they wouldn't break when he walked and it would be a little more comfortable. The boys went into the Burger King and ordered food and then went and sat down with some of the other kids who chose to eat there. Minutes later, in walks Pastor Jim and his wife and the band director. They order, they go sit down. Well, Pastor Jim gets up and goes to the bathroom. Nobody thought anything, at this point no one was really paying attention and the three adults took for granted that the boys hadn't seen them look in the trash earlier. One of the students came out of the bathroom and sat with the rest of the kids. "Ya'll, I just saw the bus driver digging through the trash. When I asked him what he was doing, he said he dropped something." Everyone all just looked at each other and kept eating.

When Pastor Jim came out of the bathroom, no one looked at him. He knew what Kyle, Jeremy, and Eric were up to and it was pissing him off that he couldn't bust them, which they had to admit, started to become funny after a while, but the boys didn't want to get too proud of themselves. They weren't out of the woods yet. The kid from the bathroom, trying to be a smart-ass, asked Pastor Jim if he found what he was looking for. To which Pastor Jim replied, "Yes, I found it. Thank you." It was too close for comfort.

After all the kids ate, they put up their trays, grabbed their sodas and left. The band director, Pastor Jim and his wife stayed behind because they were still "eating." Basically, they were strategizing the next plan of attack. Kyle, Jeremy, Eric, and Melanie walked back to the bus with a few of the girls. Apparently, the boys weren't the only ones who had snuck some contraband onto the bus. When they got back to the bus, the girls pulled out some cigarettes and lit up. The bus was positioned perfectly. On the driver's side was an open gas station lot. On the other side was a huge hedge that towered over the space between the bus and itself, providing complete blackness. No one could see the students standing in the middle, but the students could see them.

Kyle pulled out a Black and Mild. To which one of the black

girls, Anisha, said, "He got some Black and Milds. Have you ever had a shot-gun before?"

"No. What's that?" He looked confused.

"Let me see that." So Kyle handed her his cigar and she flicked the lit end until it had no ash, but was completely bright red. Then, she put the lit end in her mouth and stuck the filter end up to Kyle's nose. She cupped his face with her hands and blew the smoke into his nose. Kyle blew a ton of smoke out of his mouth and some was coming back out of his nose. It was odd, because after he coughed his ass off, he started to get this buzzed sensation. Anisha took it out of her mouth and said, "It'll get you fucked up. You got another one of those for me?" To which Kyle immediately handed the pack to her.

"You only got two left." She took one.

"Don't worry about it, it's yours." Kyle waived his hand and coughed again.

"Thank you." She handed him back his pack and the lit cigar. Then everybody wanted a shot-gun, even the kids that didn't smoke. The other black girl was pretty and used to be a cheerleader until she got tired of it. Her name was Tina. She knew how to give shot-guns as well, so Kyle just gave her his cigar and lit up the last one. Now, there were three Black and Milds being passed around the group of ten kids. Everyone was doing shot-guns. The kids stood around like they were impatiently waiting on a hit of crack. "Ooh, me next! Ooh, me next!"

But wait...I forgot to tell you how Kyle almost got caught.

Well, when Kyle went to go to dump his tray at Burger king, the pack of Black and Milds slipped from the waistband of his boxers, down his pants leg, and rested into the top of his shoe, behind the tongue. He had to walk around the restaurant purposely trying not to bend or move his leg too much for fear that the pack would fall out onto the floor. Luckily, he made it past Pastor Jim. He walked outside with the rest of the kids, where he pretended to tie his shoe, picked up the pack and put it in his pocket this time.

Later, when the bus made it back to campus at four in the morning, everyone got off and went to their cars to go home, except for Jeremy and Eric. Kyle didn't think anything of it. He just thought they were being slow about putting up their instruments in the band room. He and Melanie got in his truck and left.

Jeremy called Kyle later on that day and told him: *"Remember when I said to take everything off the bus because they were going to check our stuff?"*

"Yeah?" Kyle felt a sense of dread.

"Well, dipshit had a can of Skoal in his backpack and he didn't take it out."

"What a dumbass."

"Oh, it gets worse. Since he's not even sixteen yet and we're both seventeen, they naturally assumed that one of us had to buy it for him."

"You didn't?"

"Yep, I went to the gas station before we left for the game and got it for him. I actually bought it for me too, but he wanted it, so I just gave it to him."

"So now what?"

"Well, since they didn't find anything else and it's only dip and I am seventeen, I have to either take a suspension or a paddling on Monday. And they called my mom."

"Oh God, did she freak out?"

"Actually no. She thought it was funny. I didn't get in trouble,

so I don't care. I'm just going to take the paddling and be done with it."

"You didn't tell them about anything else, did you?"

"Fuck no, I ain't getting in any more trouble and I told Eric to keep his fucking mouth shut about it or I'd kick his ass."

"That'll work, and he also doesn't want to get in any more trouble either."

"True."

"Was my name brought up?"

"Nope."

"Whew! Thank God. I can't believe we got away with all of it. Well, most of it anyhow. But it was fun."

"Yeah, it was. Something to remember."

"Yeah, I'm sure we'll be talking about it at out ten-year reunion."

"Okay, I just thought I'd give you the heads up. If anyone asks, just say you don't know anything."

"Yeah, no shit. Later."

"Peace." Jeremy hung up.

Kyle always thinks about that night when he smokes behind the coach's office now. He put his cigarette out in the gravel and lifted it up to make sure it was completely out and then threw the butt into the dumpster. Coach Bradfield still hadn't shown up yet. He walked back inside the locker room and sat on one of the benches. The only people who had P.E. first period were the girls, so the locker room was always vacant and quiet, not like usual. It was boring. Rows and rows of old lockers. Smelly bathroom stalls. A shower system that had to be from the 1950's. *You'd think with all the money this school makes off of sports, they could clean up the locker rooms. Perhaps buy some new athletic equipment,* he thought.

Kyle picked up his Spanish book and started thumbing through it, then decided to put it back down. "See, I could've slept in." He said to himself. "This is bullshit."

Kyle paced back and forth and then walked out of the locker room into the back hallway that separated the stage and the locker rooms. He remembered being in the play the Spring before. His choir director was co-directing the play with the drama teacher and Kyle was asked to play the "jock," naturally. He only had two lines in the whole play. He basically would show up, walk across the stage, the other cast-mates would stare in awe of the hot "jock" that they're all in love with and that was it. At the end of the play, he told the girl, who was majorly crushing on him, that she did a good job or something. She gushed, he smiled. That was it. It was a simple play, but what do you expect for a small Baptist community? They might as well be Amish. Kyle was surprised they had running water and electricity.

The main reason he decided to do the play was because Melanie was going to be involved somehow, so that meant they would be able to spend more time together. Also, he talked some of the other kids into doing it as well—ya know, as a way to get out of class. Ulterior motives, yes, but motivation none the less—what else were they gonna do? It was the end of the school year.

What Kyle didn't count on was all the practices. He had just gotten done with basketball season. Track season had just began practice, which techniqually anyone who played varsity sports were "encouraged" to at least go to the four-week practice before the first meet, just "to keep up that athletic ability." Then play practice started the week after that was over. And since it was junior year, it was their turn to decorate for the senior and junior prom. The juniors had to put it on for the seniors or else they had to pay heavily to go. So everyone who didn't want to pay fifty to seventy-five dollars had to work. Now this also included the four games that the juniors each had to work in the concession stands at the football and basketball games. Needless to say, Kyle worked all his four at the football games. Still, it just seemed to be one thing after another. All this practicing, all this preparation, and for what? A few hours. Sometimes, it just didn't seem worth it.

Kyle's parents never showed up for the play, or Junior prom, or any of his games including Homecoming. His dad was never around, so Kyle always expected him to be a no-show. Mrs. Harper, however, always complained that sitting on the bleachers hurt her back or she was too tired or she had a "date." After a while, it didn't bother him. He had his things and they had theirs. As long as they were still footing the bill for everything, he stayed out of their hair. Honestly, it was easier that way. Kyle did pretty much whatever he wanted within reason, and no grief from the parental units. It was a win-win.

Of course, Kyle was kind of jealous of the other kids, who had parents that were completely supportive and involved in their lives. Sure, he had freedom but he was mostly lonely a lot of the time. Kyle also figured that was the reason he and Melanie got along so well. She was an outsider living with a family that wasn't hers, he could totally relate.

Chapter 2
(Monday night)

The lady in the red dress began her journey as her coal black eyes fixated on the path that she must walk. She walked with her head locked forward, never once looking at the dark, blanket-wrapped baby in her arms. The air lifted from the ground, swirling harvest leaves at her feet, creating a cyclone of orange and brown death as she took each step. The sky darkened. Clouds created a foggy smoke behind her, erasing her origin. Where she comes from, no one knows. But she's here now.

The crowd anxiously awaits. They watch in awe as the fog ushers her in. She walks on the leaf-covered concrete, down the center as they stand in dutiful silence.

The baby never cries, doesn't whimper, can't breathe an utterance, only looks at the raven-haired woman carrying him to his death.

The sky above her is a spectacular sight for the child to behold. Flickers of light crack the glass of darkness. Blue electric bolts cascading in sequential order creating a mirror in the infant's eyes. He raises his wax hands to touch the fire only to find his efforts melting in vain.

He touches his mother's face. Her moon-colored flesh glows around the outline of his tiny fingers. He slaps her repeatedly only to receive a blink as a response. He places his fists to his mouth, suckling his knuckles. The salty flavor makes him salivate and squint.

His mother never changes pace. One step after another. In front of the eyes of the town. They close the circle behind her and begin to follow as she makes her journey down the pavement. She leads an army of faceless eyes, ever-watching, studying, adoring…

The male offspring looks but cannot see. This hateful visage carries his body face up, never changing positions due to weary arms, never relaxing her grip.

The child's belly cramps due to lack of nourishment from his mother's teat. A muffled moan escapes behind his hands, and then a wail is let out to let her know to feed what she has not.

The people come closer. Picking up the pace to hear the child, to see what they fear. *Is it prophecy? Is it the work of the Devil?*

A familiar woman with an angelic face meets the young mother in her path. "Bless you child," she smiles. "He thanks you for your offering."

The mother stands still; she shifts her gaze down to the burden that she has been carrying. "Blessed Be."

The familiar woman steps forward and removes the babe from her rigid tentacles. The women in the crowd somberly march in succession past the still mother and follow the elder lady as she progresses further down the road. The mother's face and body turn to a skeleton as she collapses and smacks her bones on the street.

31

The boy, feeling for a breast on the old woman, only finds dry milk; an endless search to stop the hunger that cannot be fed. He feels his body lifted to the sky that he wanted so badly to touch. Moving his hands, he controls the heavens. The ether obeys his every command, yet his delight abruptly comes to an end as he is placed in the center of the circle of virgins and wives, wingless, falling from sky to earth.

The ladies come closer, tightly weaving the circle. The baby sees cloud-like faces, smiles spread wide, and a flicker of light across the amethyst above. He raises his hands one more time, trying to control what isn't there anymore. All is still.

He lowers his tiny, empty hands as the circle of ladies begin to stomp.

***

"Uhhhhhhhhhhhhhhh!" Kyle beat on his chest for oxygen to enter his lungs. He immediately rolled off the bed onto the floor gasping for air. "Uhhhhhhhh!" "Uhhhhhhh!" A painful moan escapes his throat as tears flood from their sockets.

"Kyle?! Are you alright in there?" Mrs. Harper yelled from her bedroom.

No response, just the sound of Kyle choking and groaning. "Kyle?!"

"I…uhhhhh…can't…uh…uh…uh…breathe!" Kyle rubbed his chest as it heaved in and out. He could feel his heart pound a rapid, panicked pulse. It felt like it was trying to punch through and high-five his hand.

Kyle pulled himself back up onto his bed and flopped onto his back. The cool pillow of sweat behind his head engulfed his cranium like a wet rag. He laid there staring at the pale white ceiling, breathing heavily. He was up now. *There was no point*

*in going back to sleep tonight, he might as well turn the lights
on and try to do some homework or watch TV or get a glass of
chocolate milk. He could straighten up his room, go through
letters, papers, random junk and just throw it all away. Clean.
Less clutter would be better.*

Kyle began to organize the cologne bottles on top of his
dresser. *Put the Gucci in the back. Calvin Klein in front of
those. Ralph Lauren in front of those. And the smaller bottles
in the front. No, that's not good. Taller bottles in the back,
then medium, then small. And space them all accordingly in a
concave shape so you can see every bottle.* He wiped some dust
off the front of the dresser. "I need to dust and get this all clean.
I'll put the cologne bottles to the left in a half circle, then wallet,
keys, money, change, watch." That was good and precise. Kyle
felt a sense of accomplishment and let out a proud exhale.

Turning around to eye the rest of his room, Kyle thought the
next best place to start would be the book shelf. *It really did
need to be organized. Some things didn't belong on a book shelf
and should be put in a box in the closet or simply thrown away.*
He eyed a red, remote-controlled Porsche his uncle had given
him when he was ten. Still in the box. Still in the Styrofoam.
Every once in a while Kyle would take it out of the box and
drive it around the room. The headlights worked. The top was
a detachable targa top. There was even a horn that went "beep,
beep." It was a sharp little Carrera. Kyle always told himself
that one day he would have this car, exactly like it, if not, then
some other candy apple red convertible. He imagined what it
would be like to take the top off and just drive. No destination.
No plans. A cool breeze. A cool station on the radio. Driving
off into the sunset. Through the hills. Past the farms. Past the
fields. Sipping on a Cherry Coke or Cherry-Banana Dr. Pepper
from Sonic. Him and him alone, no one else in the car with him.

Even in his happiest of states, Kyle always knew he was better off by himself. Every once in a blue moon, he would think of the "ten years from now, and where would he be" question. It always seemed so trite to even try and comprehend that far ahead in the future. Kyle always wanted to know about "the right now." That's what mattered. *He could wish his life away and never be surprised, never be thrilled, never be excited, never be happy. But since that's where he saw himself in ten years, then that's exactly where he was supposed to be? That was just too much pressure, and if he already knew the end result, then why try at all. It's all going to go according to plan, someone else's plan.*

The thought of being married and settling down to raise a bunch of kids in his twenties, before he had the chance to explore, the chance to find true bliss, the opportunity to establish the life that he always wanted…Kyle never understood why people would give up their youth, right when they're suppose to take the world by storm, right when they're suppose to make big mistakes and recover from them without inflicting any damage onto another person. *People just seem to give up on themselves way too early in life and focus too much energy on someone else that doesn't deserve it.* He wondered if that was the reason his parents split up, why his mother cheated on his father, why his dad moved so far away and remarried. *If they would have waited, maybe they would have been happy without bringing him into the middle of it all. Of course, this meant that he would never have existed. Maybe that would have been for the best.*

Kyle picked up the box and looked at the car through the plastic cover. He took it over to his closet and opened the door. He pulled the hanging string for the light and placed the car at the very back of the top shelf and pulled the string again to turn the light back off.

There weren't many books on the three shelves. In fact, there was only one row of books. The other shelves were cluttered with random stuff: workbooks from previous years in school, Mad Magazines, GQ Magazines, a snow globe, a trophy for little league which wasn't his, a gold trophy for top seller of popcorn for The Boy Scouts which *was* his, and a shoe box of pictures, baseball cards, basketball cards, playing cards, a miniature bible, make that two miniature bibles, a yo-yo or four...rubber bands, and an old note he got back Freshman year from Melanie. He forgot he had it. Must not have been all that important, but he still kept it. It wasn't the first or anything special. He just never threw it away. It went in the box along with everything else.

Kyle decided that the only things he would throw away were the mysterious little league trophy, the GQ Mag's, and the old workbooks; everything else, he would straighten up and get all the dust off of. *Of course, he really didn't need any of the stuff in the shoe box. He had a real bible, what was the point of have two miniature ones? The pictures were of a family and friends that really didn't exist anymore, no point in keeping memories of that. The baseball and basketball cards weren't part of his vast collection...the yo-yos might be fun; they were the good, expensive ones.* He had a butterfly, one that lit up red, white, and blue when it span, a classic Duncan, and his favorite, a solid wood Duncan. He couldn't get rid of that one. The others were kind of banged up from doing "around the world," "walk the dog," "Spider-Man web extension," and a bunch of other crazy things that would either slam against the wall by accident or take out the ceiling fan lights. Oops. *The letter from Melanie was nothing as well. The whole box was trash, except for the wooden Duncan.*

Kyle piled everything on top of the shoe box and carried it

out of his room, down the hall, down the stairs, into the kitchen, and tossed it all in the trash can. "Now, that's done…time for a midnight, well, 3 a.m. snack." He opened the fridge and grabbed a jug of milk. "God, why does she always buy vitamin D?"

"Because I like vitamin D." Mrs. Harper flicked on the kitchen light. "What's wrong, can't sleep?"

"No, so I decided to clean my room and throw away some stuff."

"Wow, maybe you should have sleepless nights more often, you could clean the whole house." She grabbed the milk jug from him. "Sit. I'll fix us a sandwich."

"Okay." Kyle walked to the other side of the island and sat on a stool. "So why are you awake?"

"Because you woke me up with all the noise." She grabbed a loaf of Wonderbread out of the bread box.

"Sorry. Bad dream."

"What did you dream about?"

"I don't really remember." He lied. "It was just one of those dreams that shocked me and I woke up and I couldn't breathe."

Mrs. Harper pulled a butcher knife from the wooden holder and began slicing a tomato remarkably thin. Her sandwiches were like art. She would layer lettuce, tomato, red onion, whatever meat, whatever cheese, then whatever dressing. After she was done, the sandwich would be piled high, and if that weren't enough, she would lightly grease a skillet and sear the bread. She would then slice the sandwich diagonal, spread it apart on a plate and pour chips in the middle. Then she would either garnish with a pickle or speared olives. This magic would all seem to take place in a matter of seconds. It always looked so good that you didn't want to eat it, but it was so good that you immediately scarfed it down. Kyle always thought she missed her calling of being a deli owner or having a small sandwich shop. Something good.

Mrs. Harper passed Kyle his plate and poured them both a glass of milk. "I'll get you some skim next time I go to the store, but I'm still getting mine too." She put the milk back in the fridge and carried the two glasses over and sat next to him.

"Did you ever work in a restaurant?" Kyle said with a full mouth.

"Why do you ask?"

"I don't know, you just seem to have a niche for this kind of stuff."

"Years of practice." She took a big bite of her sandwich. "Mmmm. Damn I'm good." She tore a paper towel of the holder and handed it to Kyle, then she tore one off for herself.

"Well, anytime you want to make my lunch, feel free."

"Vice versa, wait, I've seen what you eat, nevermind."

"Oh, ha ha."

They sat there and finished eating the rest of their sandwiches and chips in silence. This didn't seem like such an odd occurrence. The older Kyle got, the closer him and his mother became. It was normal that his father wasn't there, almost like habit. It was now her and him, and one day it would be just her, and it would be just him. Kyle guessed that eventually everyone leaves or disappears. Everyone goes it alone at one point or maybe even for the most part.

Chapter 3
(Tuesday morning)

Kyle dropped his backpack on the kitchen counter and began rifling through the cabinets for a bowl. Mrs. Harper sat on a stool at the kitchen island looking through an old issue of *Harper's Bazaar Magazine*. "Oh, if only I was the Harper that owns this magazine." She would always say when she read it.

Then Kyle would inevitably say, "But you do own that magazine."

"That's not what I meant." She would say almost unresponsive. It was banter. It was their thing. "Do you have practice today?"

"Yep."

"You mean 'yes.'"

"Yes, I have practice today."

"Shit."

"You mean 'shoot.'"

"No smartass, I mean 'shit!'"

Kyle smiled at her and decided that it would be best to go light this morning and skip the cereal for a glass of water. That would be quick and easy and he wouldn't have to sit here and listen to her be crabby about the whole situation. He poured a half-glass and leaned back against the counter looking at her.

"What?" Mrs. Harper felt his eyes on her without looking up.

"I didn't say anything."

"Yeah, but you're looking at me like you want to say something."

"I don't want to say anything. Can't I just look at my beautiful mother?"

"Ha! Okay, I know you're buttering me up for something.'"

"Nope." He chugs his water, puts his glass in the dishwasher and grabs his backpack. "I'll see ya later."

"Whoa! Why are you in such a hurry? I want you home after practice. Don't make me come looking for you." She put down her magazine.

"I will. Melanie wants to go with us to the Soybean Festival Parade, her host-parents said it was okay if it's okay with you."

"Okay. Tell her to be here by six on Thursday."

"Um, she's coming home with me after practice."

"Uh huh. You mean before I get home, yeah, nice try buddy."

"We're not gonna do anything."

"Oh, I know you're not, because she's coming over at six on Thursday." A devilish grin spread across her face.

"Fine." Kyle opened the door and began to walk out, then stopped. "You know, some parents actually trust their children."

"Those parents are stupid. Have a good day at school, learn something." Mrs. Harper picked her magazine back up. Kyle grumbled and marched out to his truck. "Trust my children, shit." She chuckled to herself.

Kyle still had a good twenty to thirty minutes before the

tardy bell rang. Today, he didn't have to give a ride to anyone. The typical ritual was to ride around Main Street before class started, but it was a little too early for all that. He decided to go to the grocery store and grab breakfast since he didn't eat at the house. The local IGA had horrible donuts, but they had the best steak, egg, and cheese and sausage, egg biscuits. Funny how no one ever bought them. Everyone would always go for the donuts. No nutritional value, tons of sugar, and bad, even when fresh, on top of that. Oh well, as long as everyone got their sugar and caffeine fix in the morning. Kyle always wanted real food. If it had to be sweet, then maybe pancakes, but he still wanted sausage or bacon, toast, eggs...sugar alone wouldn't do.

Morning time was always busy at IGA, the donut crowd for one, but also the early bird shoppers. "*Double coupons on Tuesdays and Thursdays!*" The earlier, the better the deals, or so everyone thought. All the old bitties liked to tell themselves that. Shopping carts filled to the top with heavenly bargains. Sometimes Kyle wondered if these people thought that the store would miraculously sell out later in the day or that some evil manager was going around like clock-work changing all the prices to punish the late shopper. It seemed moronic. Of course, these were the five-in-the-morning-day-after-Thanksgiving-shoppers, what else would they be doing early in the morning? Not sleeping, that's for damn sure.

Kyle stepped on the black pad that made the automatic door open. The same ladies were always checking customers out this time of morning. It was like they lived here, never a day off, always here, glued to their cash registers. Kyle walked past. The first thing was the heated glass case that had all the goodies he liked. Easy access. Then past the deli counter was the donut case, unusually mobbed or could be usual, Kyle did have an early start this morning. No matter. He didn't want any of that shit. Kyle grabbed two biscuit sandwiches and dodged around the mob over to the dairy section and grabbed a twelve-ounce carton skim milk.

"Shouldn't you be drinking vitamin D milk?" Kyle recognized the voice and turned around in shock.

"Shouldn't you be drinking bloody mary's with all your old pals?" He smirked as his dad grabbed him and hugged him.

"I see you still got your mom's smart mouth. So, how is my oldest son?"

"Yeah, I forgot that I'm not the only one anymore." Kyle watched as his dad shook his head and looked at the floor. "I'm fine. Actually, I'm on my way to school."

"How's the truck holding up? You taking good care of it?"

"Yep, it's good. Everything is good."

"Good." He squeezed his son's shoulder. "You're getting big."

"Yep." Kyle nodded. There was an uncomfortable silence. "So, well, I guess I'm gonna go. It was good to see you dad!" Kyle began to walk away. He rolled his eyes. *What an asshole?* He thought to himself.

"Hey, hold up." Mr. Harper catches up to Kyle and grabs the food and milk out of his hands and puts it on one of the shelves. "Let's go have a real breakfast, oldest son of mine." He escorts Kyle past the people looking.

"But I gotta go to school."

"Not today, you don't."

"Mom's not going to like this."

"Mom's not gonna know."

With his hands on Kyle's shoulder's, he follows behind as Kyle walks out of the IGA.

"What about my truck, won't someone see it?" Kyle protests.

"Who gives a shit? I'm your fucking father, they can suck my dick!"

"You sure you haven't had any bloody marys?"

"Not yet, and guess what, since you're damn near eighteen and all, you're going with me to the lodge for breakfast." He hopped into his Cadillac and unlocked the passenger-side door. Kyle looked around the parking lot. For some reason, he felt like he was going to get into trouble with school and his mom. *But this was his dad, how bad could it get? Plus, being able to drink with the "old boys" sounded like a hoot! Party!* Kyle smiled and quickly got in the car. Mr. Harper backed out abruptly and then squalled his tires as he took off. Kyle thought to himself, *could his dad actually be this cool?*

The new Cadillac seemed to hover above the road as they cruised down the street. His dad swung into the 4-Way Stop gas station and stopped at one of the pumps.

"Put ten dollars in it and use the good stuff. I'm gonna grab some smokes and lottery tickets." Mr. Harper easily shut the car door behind him and trotted in front of another car and went inside the gas station. Kyle dutifully did what he was told. *This was a nice car. He liked it.* He wondered if his dad's new family liked it. *Was it good enough for them or merely adequate?* He stood staring at the cars of the high school kids as they made a loop into and out of the old Junior Food Mart. Some looked down at the shiny, metallic red Cadi. A few passed the loop and seemingly glared at him as they drove by. *It's not mine.* He wanted to say. He knew he would be asked about it later. *"Why wasn't he in school that day?" "Whose car was it that he was putting gas in at 4-Way?"*

Kyle guessed it didn't matter. *His dad would take care of it. He always had everything wired. Or maybe it was just that he did whatever he wanted and didn't worry about the consequences. He was kind of a narcissist.*

Ten even. Kyle replaced the nozzle and walked around to get in the passenger side.

"Hey, hold up there chief. You drive." Mr. Harper tossed the keys to Kyle.

"Okay." Kyle ran around to the other side and hopped in. He put his seatbelt on and shut the door. His dad shuffled into the passenger side with his hand on the roof and a brown paper bag full of stuff in the other arm. He shut the door.

"Make er' smoke."

"Hells yeah!" Kyle pulled the lever down to overdrive and gunned it. The tires squalled as he damn near turned sideways in front of the loop, scaring the hell out of some sophomore girl in a small Fiero. "This car rocks!"

Mr. Harper's Cadi had everything: a sunroof, leather seats, climate control, and automatic everything, including the tape deck. It was like everything you would want on a car. Well... it wasn't convertible, but the open roof made up for that. This must have cost a lot. Kyle didn't begrudge his dad for his good fortune though. Honestly, Kyle felt like it was the consolation prize for the wife and family that he first invested in. Obviously, that didn't work. Maybe now, he could be happy and feel appreciated.

Kyle hit all four buttons on the door to roll down the windows as his dad opened the sunroof.

"Let's hear some tunes!" Kyle cranked the radio up. Quiet Riot, "Come on Feel the Noise" screamed out of the speaker. Kyle drove by waving at everyone he knew driving on Main Street.

Kyle's overall sense of well-being soon manifested itself into a feeling of insecurity. No one seemed to recognize him from their parent's farm truck or small-size sedan. They just looked confused and then turned to their passengers to discuss the odd event. Kyle began to wonder what questions he would have to answer the next day in class. It was becoming apparent that some would feel the need to expose his behavior to his teachers and even the principal, which would probably mean that his mother would get wind of it, and then she would beat the wind out of him. Whatever this was temporarily, would soon end badly.

For now, Kyle just had to live with the inevitable trouble that might be headed his way and try to enjoy this brief moment of happiness.

Kyle made a left down Asher Dr. The lodge was about a mile out of town, past the graveyard, past the old paper mill (which gave the town a great smell), past a few cotton fields and corn fields, almost to the "replacement *Haunted Woods*," but not quite.

"Turn here." Mr. Harper said as he pointed down a dirt road.

Kyle could see the big house where Elvis used to like to ride horses. His parents always told him that story whenever he would complain about the town being too small and how nothing big ever happened. No one famous ever came from here or to here. "No one but Elvis," they would say.

Kyle always imagined seeing his ghost or what it would have been like to have actually met him. Missed opportunities, like most things in life. *Elvis was here. He stood not far from where I'm driving and we all missed it. No one ever knew until it was already over.* It was kind of sad to Kyle.

Kyle admired the ranch for a bit and turned his focus back to the orange gravel.

"Okay, we're gonna make a left right here."

Kyle focused on what looked like an old barn. "This is it?" He pointed and looked at the house behind him. "But isn't this Greg Callahan's property?"

"Yes, it is."

"Where Elvis used to come and ride horses?"

"Oh, that's not true. Greg tells everybody that."

"Wow, this is kinda lame." Kyle nodded his head.

"You haven't seen the inside yet."

Kyle looked around as he pulled in beside a Chevy van. He turned off the radio and rolled up the windows. Mr. Harper closed the sunroof. "That has got to be the coolest thing ever." Kyle agreed with his father as he turned the key to off.

"Well, we're here. Are you ready?"

"Well, yeah."

"Well, okay, let's get out the car."

Kyle noticed the sound of a chainsaw when they pulled up, but now it was real apparent and screechingly loud. "What are they doing?" Kyle walked a little further and looked at the shop down by the house. He must have stopped because his legs wouldn't move. He watched as a man in a leather mask sawed through log after log. Kyle was so still that he couldn't even feel himself breathe.

"Oh, I see you've found Junior." Mr. Harper slapped Kyle on the shoulder.

"Junior?" Kyle said as he flinched.

"Yeah, that's Greg's idiot son. He's not really all there. We all give him shit over it."

"That's nice." Kyle couldn't stop watching the seamless motion of it all. It was like a hot knife in butter. Strait down, perfect cuts every time. The same size blocks every time.

"Hey Junior!" Kyle jumped as his dad yelled. "Don't slice your knee caps off!"

The masked figure let the chainsaw rest easily by his right leg as he looked right through them. Then, he raised the saw above his head and let out a thunderous roar from the beast. Kyle couldn't help but shake.

Mr. Harper squeezed Kyle with one arm and turned him in the direction of the barn look-a-like lodge. "He's the asshole that chases you through the woods."

"That guy is?" Kyle looked over his shoulder to see his masked assailant go back to his chore of chopping wood. He wondered if that would happen to his limbs if he ever got close enough to him in the woods.

"He always wears that stupid mask this time of year to freak people out. He such a buffoon." Mr. Harper opened the door and escorted Kyle inside. "Here we go."

Even the inside wasn't what Kyle expected. He thought that since this was a lodge, then obviously it wouldn't look like a barn on the inside as it did on the outside, but this looked more like a diner slash bar. There were tables with four chairs around them, a jukebox in the corner, a pool table, a dart board, and who Kyle assumed was "Mable" tending bar—there was a bar too.

Either they were late or these guys really like to drink early in the morning. There were an assortment of guys that waved from a few of the tables and four guys who turned around in their barstools as they walked in. Kyle immediately felt awkward like he didn't belong. It didn't help that the first man who stood up as they approached the bar said, "Shouldn't you be in school son?"

"I gave him a father/son day off." Mr. Harper to the rescue as always. "How you doing, Greg?" Kyle noticed he shook his hand in a weird way, not like a normal handshake. "And this is

Kyle." He patted him on the back. "Kyle, this is Mr. Callahan." They shook hands. "And that's Tom, George, Dave, and this dream-lady is Mable. Kyle waved at everyone as they said hello.

"So what can I get you sugar?" Mable looked like she would have been prettier in her younger years. She had grey streaks in her auburn-dyed hair. Her t-shirt was too tight, which made her boobs seem even bigger than what they already were. And she smacked her gum. To some of these horny old codgers, she might be considered a step-up from their fat, boring housewives. Kyle began to wonder as he looked around the room, just how many guys here has she laid. He wondered if his dad was one of them. He wondered if that was part of the initiation. . .

"Mable, we'll have two large bloody maries and two stacks of pancakes with sausage." Mr. Harper broke Kyle's train of thought.

"You got it, John."

"You a drinker, boy?" Greg looked at Kyle

Kyle shook his head. "Uh, not usually, no sir." The fat man began to chuckle to himself. "Yeah, I bet you're not." He paused as Mable sat down two large glasses full of red liquid and green vegetables sticking out the top. "Well, you will be after today. Just don't pass out. They do evil shit to you around here when ya pass out." He chuckled again.

Mr. Harper pulled the celery stick, the olives, the pepper, the lemon, the lime, and the straw out of his drink and sat them all on a beverage napkin. He sucked on the end of his straw. "Yeah Mr. Greg over here speaks from experience. Don't ya, Greg?"

"Oh piss off, John."

"You see, Greg and Junior had a couple rough nights last year after the woods." Mr. Harper leaned in as he was telling Kyle the story.

"Oh you were piss drunk too." Greg yelled.

"I didn't say I wasn't." He looked up at Greg. "Well, needless to say, I didn't pass out, but this fat fuck and his dumbass son did."

Kyle looked at the man sitting on the left side of him and watched as he began to squirm in his chair. He could tell this was making him feel uncomfortable.

"Yeah, basically, they stripped us down naked and took pictures of us. The next day when we came in, they were hanging up on the walls for everyone to see. Fuckin' assholes!" Mr. Greg took a big swig from his drink.

"Hey, I didn't do it." Mr. Harper raised his hands in defense.

"Yeah, but you were here."

"It was funny."

"It was not fuckin' funny!" Greg said embarrassingly. Mr. Harper began to laugh. "You're gonna get yours this year, John Harper, you just wait." Mr. Harper laughed even harder.

"I'm not passing out no time soon, fat boy."

Kyle didn't know whether to laugh or be scared. Mr. Callahan was becoming angry. Luckily, he grabbed his drink and went and sat at one of the tables with a few other guys. "Oh don't get mad." Mr. Harper called after him.

"Ah." Mr. Callahan threw his right hand up to wave him off.

"Fuck em'" Mr. Harper grabbed his drink and sat in the stool Mr. Callahan was sitting in.

As soon as he was settled in his seat, Mable sat down two plates with six pancakes and four link sausages on each. She placed a syrup dispenser, a ramekin of butter, and two sets of silverware between the plates. "There ya go." She smiled at Kyle as his eyes got big at the size of the pancakes. Surprisingly, they barely hid her large breasts behind them. Kyle chuckled to himself.

"Thanks Mable." Mr. Harper began to immediately spread butter all over his pancakes.

"You got it, hun." She said with a wink and began cleaning the vegetable medley he left on top of the bar. "John, you always make such a mess."

"Well, I gotta give you something to do. I wouldn't want you to get bored."

"Yeah, yeah."

"We all know what happens when you get bored. . ."

Kyle looked up from his mountain of pancakes to see Mable's lips become paper-thin as she pressed them together. *God, his dad is a bigger asshole than what he thought. He better say something to alleviate the tension in the room.* "Let me guess, you get all hyped up on caffeine and then go drag racing!" Kyle made sure he was loud enough for everyone to hear him. *Hopefully, it would change the subject to something more positive and actually be more engaging than what his dick of a dad was implying.*

"Is that what you do?" A big grin spread across Mable's worn visage.

"Yeah, just as long as no cops are around!" Still talking loud with a mouthful of hotcakes.

"Really? And just what do you drive, little man?" She finished wiping off the counter.

"A Chevy."

"Good boy. I've always been a GM over Ford kinda gal."

"Not my momma, she's exact opposite."

"And you wonder why we're divorced." Mr. Harper chimed in and took a big gulp from his bloody mary.

"Mom always said it was because you were an asshole!" Everyone within earshot laughed at that one, including Mable. What made it even more funny was that Mr. Harper choked as soon as Kyle said it. Kyle knew for sure that he was going to be in trouble when his father turned in his stool and glared at him.

"I'll agree with that." Mr. Harper shrugged it off and went back to what was left of his large stack.

Whew! Kyle thought. He was expecting to be knocked out of his chair for disrespecting his father like that, especially in front of people that he always tried to impress. Maybe that was the reason, he didn't get hit. Either way, he wasn't going to press his luck again.

Mable winked at him in congratulations as well as gratitude. Kyle smiled and went back to his bloody mary. *It was spicy as hell, but good. And all the vegetables and fruit and stuff she put in it as a garnish was cool.* It was what he expected a tropical resort type place would do. *It was also so easy to drink, not like beer, which had a nasty taste, or like whiskey or gin, which was too strong—this was good, and drinkable. He liked bloody maries. Now he had something else to talk about with his friends.*

It didn't take long for it to be "bottoms up" and the drink was gone. Kyle was surprised that he drank it so fast, even more surprised that he had beaten his father.

"You ready for another, Sug?" Mable grabbed his glass.

Kyle looked at his father and then looked at his drink. "Don't let me hold you back." Mr. Harper said without looking up from his food, but feeling the hesitation on his son's part. "Drink up; we got a long day ahead of us."

"Okay, I'll take another." He said with a big grin. "But I do need to go to the bathroom. Where is it?" Kyle got up from his stool.

"It's over by the dart board in the back." Mable nodded to her right.

"Good, I gotta pee." Kyle noticed that everyone watched as

he walked past the bar and past their tables. He guessed they were all waiting for him to stumble or go throw up. Or maybe it was weird having a high school kid in the lodge. *Who knows?*

Kyle walked past the dart board, down a little hallway to a door that said "gentlemen." Further down the hall was what he assumed was the "ladies." It just said, "Mable." *Well, a lady needs her own bathroom,* he thought. That's what his mom always said.

Kyle opened the door to the "mens" and stepped inside. When he flipped the light switch, the exhaust fan came on as well. To his surprise, the walls weren't decorated with scantily-clad pictures of naked women or the insignia of a dirty limerick master. It was simple: a condom machine, a few ducks unlimited prints, a box of tissue, and the usual porcelain appliances. Nothing gross, nothing lude, and nothing was out of place; this bathroom was cleaner than the one he had at home. *Mable must be the one that keeps things tidy around here,* he thought.

Kyle relieved himself of the water pressure that was building up in his bladder and then flushed the shiny, new toilet. "This bathroom is nice." He said aloud. He began to wash his hands and check his hair and face in the mirror. It had been awhile since he had a zit. His face usually stayed pretty clear, though he was pale a lot when he didn't get a tremendous amount of sun. His eyes seemed baggy as always. He patted some water on his cheeks and eyes. *Not enough.* He splashed his face with cupped handfuls of water. *That's better.* He turned off the faucet and reached for the hand towels to dry his face. He leaned forward more, not to drip all over the front of his shirt.

The hand towels were scratchy. They hurt his skin until the water soaked through. He rubbed his eyes softly with the damp towels, and then tossed them into the trash can by the sink. He looked back into the glass to see a face he never thought he would see. He blinked, and blinked again. . . he's dreaming again! No, it can't be a dream.

Kyle didn't realize that the loud sound coming from his throat had started long before he fully understood that Junior was behind him, watching him.

Kyle spun around and leaned back against the sink. He looked into the eyeholes of the leather mask to see if there was anything human behind it. "Why are you wearing that mask?"

No response.

"Junior?"

Still nothing.

Mr. Harper walked up behind Junior and slapped him on the back of the head. "Boy, one of these times you're gonna get shot scaring people like that." He pulled his mask off and handed it to him. "Now move. I gotta piss."

Kyle exhaled and walked past the overweight man in his plaid shirt and blue jeans. It reminded Kyle of the Brawny guy. He didn't really move, just stood there, like he was waiting.

Kyle made his way back to his seat, not making eye-contact with anyone, not knowing if they heard him scream like a little girl. He took a sip from his bloody mary. *God, the people out here are really fucked up.* He glanced around the room and then looked over at Mable who was polishing glasses, off in her own little world. *She probably has to keep her mind on something else while she's here.*

Kyle wasn't hungry anymore. He didn't really want the rest of this bloody mary either. He wasn't used to this much sugar in the morning and he definitely wasn't used to any alcohol in the morning. His stomach wasn't feeling so well at this point. Maybe it was the spice, probably the alcohol and overload on sugar, or maybe it was being scared out of his wits, now his nervousness was affecting his body. His dad still hadn't come back from the bathroom and neither had Junior.

"mmmm, cramps." Kyle murmured as he grabbed his stomach.

"You okay hun?" Mable walked over to the back of the bar, grabbed a plastic bottle, and trotted over to Kyle. "Take some antiacids. Those bloody maries will getcha if ya have a weak stomach. You'll be alright in a couple minutes."

"Sage." Kyle grunted.

"Huh?"

"I'm allergic to sage." He took a slow, relaxed breath. "The sausage. You put sage in your sausage."

"You know they say sage wards off evil spirits." Mable looked at him and smiled.

"Well, my mom is allergic to sage and so was my grandma and they aren't evil."

"That you know of hun?" Mable walked back down to her glasses and to get Junior a beer. Kyle wondered what she meant by that, then noticed Junior looking at him. Kyle felt afraid and quickly turned in his chair to the bottle of antiacids sitting in front of him.

"Couldn't hurt." Kyle grabbed the bottle and fudged with it until he got it open. He shook way too many out. "Two will work." He poured the rest back in the bottle and popped the two left into his mouth. He chewed until there was this sour face that spread across his visage. "Yuck." He immediately grabbed the second bloody mary, removed all the shit floating in it, and slugged half of it down.

"And you say you ain't evil?" Mable shook her head. Kyle coughed and laughed at that one, maybe out of nervousness, maybe because it was funny.

"You seem in good spirits son." Mr. Harper came back finally and sat down beside him. "You getting drunk over here?" You know Mable only does that so she can take advantage of you in the back later." He looked over at Mable.

"Hell, you're confusing me with you, John Harper." Mable adjusted her cross necklace.

It's so obvious, Kyle thought to himself. *Time to find out.* "So how long have you two known each other."

"I grew up around John." Mable leaned against the bar.

"Yeah, she used to chase me around." Mr. Harper chimed in.

"He's full of shit. Me and your daddy were sweet on each other for a while. Well, that was until...your mom." They both looked at each other in silence. Mable looked down and began folding her bar towel. "Sometimes you just know."

"And nine months later, here you are." Mr. Harper squeezed Kyle's shoulder. He turned back to Mable. "But we always remained friends, and always will." He began eating his pancakes again.

"I'll get you another bloody mary." Mable began to walk away.

"I want a shot of tequila, and you're taking one with me." Mr. Harper turned to Kyle. "You're in too." Mable stopped and she began to smile.

"So three then?" Mable lined up three shot glasses on the bar and then looked at John and nodded like things would be okay. Kyle noticed him look at her with a longing that he never saw between him and his mother. *God, did he really love her? Then, why in the hell isn't he with her? Why did he leave town and marry some other bitch in Texas and have kids with her? I want my daddy back, dammit!* Then, the bright idea bulb exploded and before Kyle knew it, he had already said what he was thinking loud enough for others to hear. "Maybe you two should be together!"

"Out of the mouth of babes." Mable shook her head after she took her shot.

John took his shot and sat quietly. "Things change."

"No they don't. And only if you let them. It's obvious you two love each other." They both just looked at him and Kyle noticed as he looked past them that everyone else was too.

"Maybe you should just take your shot." Mr. Harper slid the shot glass in front of him. Kyle took it and began coughing and rubbing his chest. "That burn gets you every time!" He laughed and patted Kyle on the back. "You want another one?" Kyle waived in defeat "no". "Finish your pancakes, we have to go out to the woods." He got louder. And someone added a "That's right!" Kyle eventually stopped coughing after he took another swig from his bloody mary.

God, what have I gotten myself into?

Everything didn't seem so fun to Kyle anymore. *The morning had started out great and light and the next thing you know we're trolloping off to this scary ass place in the woods. Maybe it wouldn't be so bad during the daylight. Maybe if I could see what was actually there, when I had to be there at night, I would know what's actually in the dark.* Somehow it still wasn't comforting.

And now everyone was packing up their coolers (full of beer), tarps, axes, chainsaws…*what the hell was this, a party for cannibals?* Kyle was starting to feel the effects of the alcohol. "You drive." He handed back the keys to Mr. Harper.

"Feeling a little buzzed are we?"

"I just need to sit for a while, and then I'll be fine." Kyle put his seat belt on and shut the door. He started rubbing his forehead. "I'm starting to get a headache."

"Don't get sick on me now. I need you to keep it together." Mr. Harper looked at him strangely.

"I'll try dad, I'll try." Kyle closed his eyes and took a deep breath.

Chapter 4
(Tuesday Night)

Kyle laid in his bed dozing in and out as he watched *The Munsters* on *Nick at Nite*. Today wasn't too bad, other than the stomach pains, the headache, and his dad being a jerk. At least he got to see him.

Kyle's eyes started to become heavy as he fought off sleep. He kept trying to focus on what was on the screen. He blinked once. Slowly, he blinked a second time. Then everything became crystal clear. Kyle watched the black and white TV screen as it got bigger and came closer until he was absorbed into the screen. A man with clown make-up and a striped, black and white shirt pranced with his top-hat back and forth across a wooden stage. The crowd giggled and pointed as he danced and kicked, and lifted his hat. *Was this a comedy show?* Kyle thought.

Kyle looked down and noticed that he was wearing a white ruffled shirt and dark brown pants. His hair had grown longer. His face, scruffy and dirty. Yet, there was no sound. No sound came from the crowd as they laughed at this clown up on stage.

No sound came from the clown as he stomped and pranced. He mimed every outburst and they…they cheered him along. Not in Technicolor, in black and white.

As the wind blew, the clown pretended to be blown way back. He leaned forward. He portrayed to struggle against the mighty gusts. The crowd silently applauded and cheered.

Six ropes swayed back and forth in the breeze behind the clown on stage. They reminded Kyle of a tire-swing rocking from side to side as each breath from God gave them momentum. The clown stomped around behind the ropes. He grabbed the first and held up his index finger in front of his followers for them to take a pause. He then diligently began twisting and turning and knotting; all the while making faces, looking at the accidentally on-purpose mistakes he was making. When he got finished, he took an over-exaggerated breath, heaving his shoulders up and down. Then, he held his masterpiece before the people. A perfectly, knotted noose.

Massive cheers and applause. This man had really outdone himself. "Such effort. Such detail." "What a talent. What an artist." "How wonderful." The people mouthed the words as the clown took a bow and moved onto the next rope, and then the next, and then the next…until all six were at perfect length, perfectly cylindrical. They were beautiful. "A masterpiece." "Superb." The people all clapped vigorously.

The clown waved his hands like it was no big thing. He placed his right hand to his chest and looked away like he didn't deserve their praise. He smiled and took a congratulatory bow, holding his top-hat out before him. He quickly arose and stammered over to the first piece of art he hand-made and stuck his head through the opening. He held the top above his head and pulled it taught. Then he closed his eyes and stuck his bright red tongue out. His audience loved it. At this point, they loved him. *How entertaining this man was.*

Kyle watched in horror as the clown stuck his head in each noose and made the same expression. No matter how upsetting the cheers and applause from the people around him were, he couldn't take his eyes off what was taking place up on the platform in front of him. *It was grotesque.* He stood in awe, watching breathlessly, waiting to see what was going to come next.

Once again, the clown stopped. He raised his hands for the audience to hush. He then turned sideways, took a bow with his left arm stretched out, and began to back up; introducing his assistants. **Sarah Goode**. She waved and smiled at the people and then stepped up and put her head through the first noose. **Rebecca Nurse**. One by one they walked out merrily and did the same. **Susannah Martin**. **Elizabeth How**. **Sarah Wildes**. They were stars for the evening. They were there to receive recognition and to help entertain the masses, just as the clown does. "What an honor," a strange woman said.

The ladies in their beautifully layered dresses filled up the first five nooses, leaving one on the end to blow easily in the wind. The clown crossed his arms and started tapping his foot. He placed his forefinger to his cheek and looked to the heaven in contemplation. Then…Suddenly…An a-ha moment! The clown raised his forefinger in exasperation. Eyes wide. Mouth opened. He needed a volunteer from the audience!

But not just any volunteer, no. The volunteer had to be worthy. This was a special prize for a special person. It couldn't be just bestowed upon anyone, no. This was recognition. This was fame. This was a cultural event that would be studied and talked about for centuries to come. This person would go down in history as one of the select few.

Not only did he need another worthy assistant, but the clown needed to make a statement. He needed "The non-believer." The one who would not be tainted. The one who did not believe in magic or the cultish ways of the feeble-minded townsfolk. The clown needed a true "smarty-pants." A buffoon. The one on the outside looking in and reminding everyone that it's all a lie. The town. The church. The little accusing bitches who will forever burn in hell for what they've caused. He needed...that guy!

The scene drew back until every head had followed the pointing finger back to **Kyle Harper**. Kyle froze. The clown motioned with his arm for Kyle to come up on stage with the other beautiful assistants. Behind the clown, the ladies were motioning with their hands for Kyle to do the same. Then, the audience began to push. They began to wail and prod, until Kyle was standing before them. Between *them* and the stage. Between *them* and judgment. Between *them* and infamy.

He stood as hands pressed into his back moving him closer. The clown lent him a helping hand. Kyle looked up at the white made-up face with deep black circles around the mouth and eyes. He looked like a skeleton, no longer a clown. He aggressively grabbed Kyle's wrist and pulled him up on stage. *He was so strong.* Kyle felt like a child that had been lifted up by his father, out of the abyss.

The clown guided Kyle to the last loop and began to motion with his right arm for the audience to cheer and applaud his efforts. Kyle stood by the happy women with a blank stare on his face and a tear of acid hotly streaming down to his chin. The clown placed Kyle's head through the loop and snuggly tightened the knot. He looked at Kyle and then looked at crowd. The clown puckered his bottom lip and began to fake rub his eyes with his fist. The crowd laughed. The clown laughed. Even the other assistants laughed.

The crowd was ready. They were waiting on pins and needles for what was to come next. *Would he do it all at once? Would he do it one at a time? Who would be first? Which end would he start at? Would he pick and choose? And who was going to be last?* The anticipation was killing them. Never before had there been such a show, such a display. They were truly lucky to be alive and in this moment. They were God's children and he was blessing them for all their hard efforts and constant praise. This was their reward. A show like no other. A show to end all shows. Live Entertainment! Live Death! Now they would get to see the true face of God. Now they would get to see his true nature. This was beauty. This was truth!

The clown ran and slid to the other side of the platform. He walked up to Sarah Goode and placed his elbow on her shoulder and began to lean on her. He smoked an imaginary pipe with his right hand. He blew out a fake smoke ring and pretended to touch it. The audience loved it. "What a performer." "He's such a stitch." After he and Sarah both had a jolly laugh along with the audience, the clown bumped her hip with his and sent her plunging below. Her rope immediately grew stiff like a harp's cord. The crack of the twisting rope on the wood it was hanging from sounded sickening, like the tree was groaning, saddened at what it had been made to do.

Besides Kyle, the tree was the only being that felt a sense of melancholy, much less remorse. Kyle struggled with the knot to tear himself free…to get away from these people… to run into the woods, away from God, away from the town's punishment. But the clown would never let that happen. He was a messenger from the almighty, put into place to entertain the town with his sermons. To make them feel something inside of their hollow existence. If not for him, they would have to entertain themselves, and they would do it all wrong!

The clown made **Sarah Wildes** hold Kyle's rope tightly so he could not get away. He lifted the hand of **Elizabeth How** up to Sarah's rope. Then he did the same with **Susannah Martin**, and then **Rebecca Nurse**, until there was a chain linking each assistant to the next.

The clown broadly walked by showcasing his next knot, his next trick to the audience. Oh, they loved it. "What a genius." "Let the sins that group them together lead them to their fate." "Magnificent. How does he come up with such brilliance?"

The clown meekly strolled down to Kyle's end with his hands up, like he did nothing wrong. This was out of his hands. He had no part in this situation. He was just a mediator at the mercy of the crowd. This was at the request of the voyeurs that wanted to watch. He walked back down to the other end, hands still up. He made his way around the first rope (bink, bink on the harp's cord), then to the back of **Rebecca Nurse** and placed his cold digits of death on her shoulders. He leaned his head over her shoulder and looked down into the pit. With a big smile on his painted face, he looked at the crowd to gauge their reaction. Of course it was funny. Of course. It was hilarious.

They waited, quietly…and then, with a small push on Rebecca, there went one. Then Susannah, then Elizabeth, then Sarah, then ultimately Kyle. The audience jumped and clapped in adoration. The **"Knot of Death"** trick worked. "Glorious." The assistants were all still holding on to one another even at the bottom as they swung together like children playing in the yard.

The clown took a bow.

Kyle sobbed into his pillow after he woke up. "That was so awful. When is this ever going to stop?"

Mrs. Harper flicked the light switch on. "Kyle, what's

wrong?" She came and sat on the bed and wrapped her arms around him as he began to hyperventilate.

"These stupid nightmares! They won't stop!" He coughed up some phlegm and wiped his eyes.

"It's because of your dad, isn't it?"

Kyle didn't say anything. He didn't want her to know that he saw him today and that he skipped school.

She rocked him back and forth. "I know this hasn't been an easy transition on you. It hasn't really been easy on me either. It's hard not seeing him and he's been gone for so long."

Was that remorse that he heard in her voice? Kyle thought. *Who the hell was she talking to? He can't breathe at this current moment but yet he's supposed to feel some sort of sympathy for her. What a bitch!*

"I'm fine." Kyle pushed her away. "I'm going back to sleep." He rolled over and fluffed his pillow under his head.

She didn't say anything. She took a moment and looked at him, then got up and walked over to the door. She paused as he closed his eyes. There was nothing to say; only flick the lights off and go back to bed.

Chapter 5
(Wednesday Afternoon)

Kyle sat completely still, only the robotic movement of his neck turning as Pastor Jim drudged past his pew showed any sign of awareness. "Why is he dressed like that?" Kyle leaned over and whispered to his mother.

"I don't know, maybe he didn't have anything else to wear." Mrs. Harper bowed her head and closed her eyes.

Pastor Jim didn't look at the singing choir as he climbed the steps to the podium. His stature was over-powering, like he was guided by God, or Satan. He turned to face the congregation but didn't look up.

"What's he doing?"

Kyle's mom looked up. "Maybe he's praying before he starts his sermon. Shhh." She placed her forefinger to her lips.

The stoic figure in black looked like an angel of death as he raised his hands. The choir began to quiet. When Mrs. Gerdy didn't stop playing, he shot her a red-eyed glare that made her turn completely pale. Kyle watched as she slowly lifted her hands from the keys. "What the hell was that about?"

Mrs. Harper spatted his right leg. "Don't swear in church." She whispered.

"Look." He pointed to the front of the church. All was quiet and the preacher still wasn't saying anything. The silence was deafening and causing Kyle's heart to race. *How long was this going to last,* he thought, *before he says anything?* He took a hard gulp as his mother squeezed his hand. "Something's wrong, isn't it?"

His mother didn't say anything or acknowledge his question. He sat there uncomfortably exchanging glances with the other parishioners, possibly thinking the same thing he was. He shrugged along with the older man sitting in the pew across from him. Obviously, no one else knew what was going on either.

Pastor Jim didn't raise his head, he just began speaking: "All of my life, I have followed the word of God and have been guided by his hand. But I have failed. I have failed myself and I have failed God." He took a long pause.

"The people of this town have sinned!" Everyone in the church jumped. "They've sinned against God and they have sinned against their fellow man!" He slammed his fist down on his Bible. "This is no longer a house of worship. It's a house of repentance! Now, I want you all to take a moment and let that sink in. I want you to sit there in silence and think! Think about the sins that you've committed this past week! Think about the sins you've committed this past month! And when you are done..." He took a quiet breath. "When you feel like you've atoned for your sins, then get up quietly and go home."

Pastor Jim left his Bible on the podium. He stepped down from the pulpit, not looking at anyone and walked out the back door. The congregation jumped again as the door slammed loudly behind him.

Muffled cries and sniffling could be heard over the hush of

the crowd. Kyle's mom became overwhelmed with emotion and ran out of the church sobbing. No one looked at her. Everyone just sat there motionless until one of the deacons stood and shouted, "This is blasphemy! How dare he condemn us to hell when he is just as much of a sinner as we are?!"

"Harvey!" His wife scolded him.

"I don't care! You can sit here all you want; I'll be in the car!" He stomped out with his hat on. Eventually, people began to follow his lead and left grumbling to themselves.

What would make Pastor Jim so angry? Kyle thought to himself. *He said the people of this town. Did he mean all of us? I haven't done anything. I mean I know that I'm no saint, but I'm not a sinner like he suggests. He must have been talking about someone else. Had to have been.* Kyle looked at everyone as he was walking out. *Maybe he was talking about one of them.* He scanned the crowd. *Someone here did something really bad and Pastor Jim knows about it. I wonder who it is. You all look guilty, but one of you did something, I know it.*

"Did you notice how he said he failed God first, before he mentioned us?" Jeremy Black stepped up behind Kyle.

"Yeah, I caught that. Sounds like someone has a guilty conscience."

"Yeah, no shit. Which I never believe these preacher types are as perfect as they claim to be. They're human just like we are." Jeremy skidded his shoes as he walked along the sidewalk with Kyle.

"I don't even know why we go to church anymore. I mean, we've read this stupid book fifty million times. I want to harp on something else for a change."

"I can see that."

"It is kinda weird that he's doing this the week of Halloween." Kyle stopped

"Yeah, and with all the stories about a virgin Christian being sacrificed to Satan at *The Haunted Woods* on Halloween."

"Huh?"

"You didn't hear? There's this satanic cult. They've been painting pentagrams on buildings at the river. They've been killing animals. Now, they're going to kill a human so the Devil will bless them."

"You're so full of shit."

"No, I'm serious. That's what we talked about at the last youth rally. The sheriff was there and everything. They told us to be on the look out and to not go to *The Haunted Woods* on Halloween. It would be best if we didn't go out at all on Halloween. They're even talking about burning down churches."

"Sounds like anarchy."

"Sounds like a bunch of bullshit if you ask me. Just another scare tactic to keep us from throwing eggs or TP'ing someone's house."

"Yeah, but that seems to be a bit of an overkill, don't ya think?"

"As long as it gets the point across, these stupid adults will do anything."

"And they say we lie!" Kyle chuckled to himself.

"I know. So where did you're mom go? I saw her leave crying."

"Yeah, she's overly emotional at this time of year with dad and all."

"I don't think I ever met your dad."

"Oh, he'll show up every once in a blue moon. He was already gone when you moved here."

"Where did he go?"

Kyle stopped. "Shhh. Here comes mom." Jeremy pretended

they were talking about something else. "Well, I'll see you at school tomorrow!"

"Yeah, lata!"

"You're so not smooth." Mrs. Harper walked past him towards the car. "Get in the car."

Kyle dutifully followed, after he looked around, almost embarrassingly, to see if anyone had heard. Nope. He was in the clear. Mrs. Harper slammed the car door after she got in. "Oh shit." Kyle mumbled to himself.

Kyle lightly shut the door as he got in and began fastening his seatbelt.

"So, did you have fun on your day off?"

"My day off?" He tried to play it off, but he knew exactly what she meant, and that only seemed to anger her more.

"Mhmm. So you have no idea what I'm talking about?" She straightened her glasses on her face. Kyle thought he was about to be hit.

"Yes." Kyle said solemnly. "I didn't mean to, but you know how it is with dad and all. It's a lot of pressure."

"You use that way too much as an excuse to get out of doing what you're suppose to be doing."

"No I don't."

"Yes, you do." She started the car and slammed the stick into drive. Kyle was waiting for her to squeal the tires and make an even bigger scene in front of all the church people, but she smoothly eased out onto the street and drove like everything was fine.

"You act different around this time of year, too." Kyle tried pushing his point.

"Son, let me tell you something. When you become an adult and you get married and have children, then you can make all the decisions and mistakes that you want. But until that day happens, I suggest you drop it!" Mrs. Harper began picking up speed. Kyle sat looking out the window wondering how much easier his life would have been if things were the opposite... if he was with his dad...instead of her. *Life would have been so much better.*

Chapter 6
(Thursday Afternoon-Parade Day)

Kyle sat in the locker room reading "Our Town."

"What's up, Nerd!?" Eric Wilson knocked the book out his hand. Kyle just sat there, zoning out as the pages flipped when the air from the fan blew over them. "Dude, are you sick? You look like you're going to throw up or something."

"It's just odd." Kyle threw his duffle bag into the locker and pulled out his button-down Polo shirt.

"What is?" Eric took his towel off and hung it over the locker door.

"Ghosts."

"Oh is that what the books about?"

"Yeah, this town is like haunted by all these people. It's weird."

"Sounds like Waterville."

"Basically. So you going to the parade?" Kyle pulled up his blue jeans.

"Yep." Jeremy pulled out a container of baby powder and started dousing his groin area.

"You shake it more than three times, you're playing with it."

"I just love the way it feels when I massage it in." Jeremy began exaggeratingly stroking himself and laughing.

Kyle stood up and waved his hand while coughing. "God, that shit chokes me. My mom wears that powdery smelling shit. Ugh."

"Keeps me from rubbing myself raw."

"Well if you quit stroking yourself…"

"Yeah, but what fun would that be?" Eric sat the powder on the top shelf of his locker.

"True."

"I'm definitely going to *The Haunted Woods*, but I don't know about the parade."

Kyle zipped up his pants and buttoned the fly. "I don't really have a choice."

"Dude, why so somber. It's gonna be a fuckin' hoot!" Eric balled up his towel and threw it at Kyle's head. Kyle ducked.

"Aw, too slow. No wonder you're on Junior Varsity."

"Yeah, I got you're junior hanging right here." Eric grabbed his package and tugged at it like he was shifting gears on a straight six.

"Now see that's why you're raw, too much hand-eye coordination on your dick." Kyle began lacing up his Nike's.

"You're just mad because yours isn't as big as mine."

"A horse's dick isn't as big as yours! You're a freak of nature dude."

"Oh come on Kyle." Eric started hunching his leg. "You know you want to touch it."

"Fuckin' gross!" Kyle pushed him back. "God! Now I'm gonna get fuckin' VD." He slapped the powder residue off his knee.

"It's the gift that keeps on giving." Jeremy chuckled to

himself as he put on a pair of white briefs and a t-shirt. "I'll probably see ya somewhere in between."

"Cool. Well, I'll see ya later." Kyle shut his locker and leaned over and picked up his book off the floor. "Our town. Huh, I guess the name's appropriate."

"Huh?" Eric pulled up his pants.

Kyle turned around. "Um, nothing. I'll see ya later." He waved the book and left the locker room.

The town always seemed like it had more people during fall festivities, Kyle noticed. Random people came out of the woodworks and they had to be from town, *why else would they come?* Other than *The Haunted Woods*, Kyle never saw what would be the draw. Honestly, he never saw why running for your life through dark woods and being blinded by strobe lights would be a draw either. *People are stupid. They do anything for a thrill, even if it's acting completely debaucherous.*

The air even seemed different, like one week it would be calm, breathable, and the next; thick, cold, active.

Kyle always got the jitters this time of year. Technically, anytime things got busier or crowded, he started shaking his leg, which drove people nuts that were sitting in the church pew with him. He couldn't help it. It was a nervous reaction to bad energy. Sometimes he would get sick to his stomach if it was too much, and he almost always had to pee. He never really understood why he was so skittish; maybe it was a "fight or flee" mechanism that set his brain off in survival mode. Maybe it was growing up in fear of the woods, fear of what was behind the shed, fear of what cannot be seen. *The Haunted Woods* had all that. No light. No hope. It was hell.

Kyle sat in the driver's seat of his truck listening to the radio. Sometimes he got tired of listening to the same tapes over and over again. The radio provided a buffer. Sure it was songs he would never buy, but every now and again they would play something decent that he didn't already have.

Kyle pushed a button and watched the orange wand jump from one side to the next, he never could figure out how to get it where he wanted. Sometimes it would be close, but most of the time he would use the knob, saved time. REO Speedwagon's "Take it on the Run" was playing, and this time it was at the beginning of the song, which never seemed to happen.

"God, I wish she'd come on. How long does it take to pick and brush her perm?" Kyle honked his horn. "I just want to get this over with."

After a few minutes Mrs. Harper came out of the front door with dark red lipstick and shiny dark brown hair. "What the fuck?" Kyle mumbled to himself.

"Why are you honking?" Mrs. Harper said as she opened the door and struggled to climb up into his truck.

"Did you die your hair?"

"Vonnie did it. Why? Do you like it?"

"I liked it better red."

"Oh, well." She shut her door and fastened her seatbelt. "Seatbelt."

"I never wear mine in the truck."

"Put it on. I'm not paying for a ticket."

Kyle did as he was told, begrudgingly, and backed out of the drive. They both waved at some of the neighbors who were outside. They were always outside, which was kinda odd considering that their house was nicer on the inside than anybody's. Maybe that's why it was. Who knows? They were

73

just those type of people; always camping, Bar-b-q-ing, playing croquette...clack! Clack!

Kyle switched radio stations as he drove down the highway. "Now, I don't want to listen to any of that heavy metal stuff." Mrs. Harper clutched her purse in her lap like an old lady. Kyle didn't say anything, clenching his jaw, chewing on his bottom lip. "Wait." She put her hand on his arm. "Leave it there."

Kyle sat back in his seat as they listened to Marty Robbins. *Nobody listens to this shit accept for old people,* Kyle thought, *really old people.* He looked at her. *Truckstop people. People who watch westerns all day on Saturday because they're too lazy to go outside. People who eat grits and liked them. People who talk about "the good ole' days." People who complain that everything is too high now and that they used to buy stuff for a nickel. People who live to visit places like Branson and The Grand Ole Opry. People who always buy American because it's cheaper. People from the war who are now shut-ins.* Kyle massaged his temple. "I got a headache."

"A head like that's suppose to ache."

He was surprised she took a moment away from reflection of farm life to notice what he said. He turned down Dante's Avenue. The tallest trees in town were on this street. The closer you got to Main Street, the more they hovered across the road creating a constant shadow.

"Park at the bank." His mom motioned for him to turn onto Third Street.

"Yeah, if it's not full." Kyle looked at all the cars lining the road. "Oh look, there's Mable." He honked.

"Who's Mable?"

"A friend of dad's"

"Really?"

"Never met her."

"How have you not?"

"I Dunno. But I've never met her."

"She went to school with you guys."

"I don't remember her."

"So dad didn't talk about any of his other girlfriends?"

"Oh, so she was a girlfriend. I see."

"What?"

"Well, it's just funny how girls like to romanticize things when someone is nice to them."

"Meaning?"

"I was his only girlfriend in high school."

"Oh. I see." Kyle could sense her tension and felt the need to stir the pot even more. "Well maybe it was before you two went out."

"I'm telling you there was no one else." She got more stern in her voice. "I don't know why women make shit up like that. I was with your father and that's it."

"Okay. Chill out! God!"

"You chill out."

Luckily there were a couple open spots at the bank. Kyle parked and hopped out of the truck. He slammed the door. Mrs. Harper was still taking her sweet time. Kyle rubbed his head again and saw his dad's Cadillac drive by. *Now if I was an asshole, I would randomly introduce Mom to Mable while she's with dad, but since I'm not an asshole, I'll leave it alone*, Kyle grinned to himself.

"You ready to go?" Mrs. Harper interrupted his train of thought. Kyle turned around to face her and smiled. "What?" She said.

"Nothing. Let's go."

"Melanie said she would meet us by the flower shop." Kyle walked a couple steps in front of his mother.

"Why are you walking so fast? The parade isn't going anywhere."

"I guess I want to get to her before she leaves."

"Why would she leave?"

"Why does everyone leave?"

His mother had no response. Kyle took a deep breath and slowed down to her pace. Everyone they walked by looked like a complete stranger: teenagers his age, little kids, people his mom and dad's age. *Who are all of these people? Blankly staring, like they have no place to go and they don't want to be here.*

Most people didn't acknowledge anyone around them. They watched their children play in front of them. They impatiently looked down the road waiting for something or someone to come: a vendor, a float, a marching band. Something. Something was coming.

Kyle and his mother crossed the street and hopped up on the sidewalk leading to Bud's Drugs. Four kids chased each other past him and his mother. The drug store had the prime location of being on the corner, next to the bank, one block down from the grocery store, close to the flower shop, close to the city diner...it became the hub of the crowd. Plus, they sold candy. They had the best suckers in town. The owner was a saint and gave so many people jobs and let them pay late on prescriptions. The line started at the back entrance and wrapped around past the front.

"Wow, this place is nuts." Kyle grabbed his mother's arm.

"It always is." She said solemnly. "Go find Melanie. I'll wait here."

"Why?"

"Because I have to pick up a prescription."

"Are you sure?"

"Yes. Go."

"Okay." Kyle turned and started cutting through the crowd of strangers. A few made a disgruntled gesture at his disturbance, but most simply stared in amusement at his passing. He was swimming through a tide that was pushing him back as hard as he was trying to get forward. Until he noticed Melanie, then the sea began to calm and the boat began to right itself. The wind was finally at his back. Another boy his age came up and put his arm around her. She kissed him on the lips as he lifted her up. Kyle's heart sank in his chest and he could once again feel the swell of the ocean as it started to carry him away. Only this time he didn't care. He let the sharks have the fish.

"You ready? Melanie's kissing on some other guy, I want to go home."

"Okay." She handed the prescription bag to Kyle as he wrapped his arm around her. "I still love you son."

"I know you do ma, I know you do."

They both walked out of the ocean of people onto the clear bank parking lot. Kyle gave her his keys. "You can drive. I don't feel like it anymore."

Chapter 7
(Friday Night)

"Where are we going?" Kyle giggled as he chased Melanie across the front yard into the two story white house. The sun seemed so bright outside. The white clothes that they were wearing seemed to glow and almost have a blinding effect.

"I want to play a game. Come on."

Kyle followed behind as she opened the front door and disappeared into the house. "Should we be in here?"

"It's okay. I won't tell." Melanie laughed and ran down the hallway into the kitchen. Then, she was out the backdoor, across the back porch and into the back yard.

Kyle stopped in the back doorway and looked back into the kitchen. *This seemed like a nice house*, he thought. He wondered who used to live here, how big their family was, did they have children? The kitchen was decorated with white and blue tile countertops, white-washed cabinets and a white linoleum floor. Kyle imagined sitting at the table having breakfast. A big stack of pancakes with a dollop of fresh butter melting across the top. A glass of milk. A glass of orange juice. He could almost smell the sausage patties cooking. His dad sitting at the head of the table reading the paper, drinking his morning coffee. His mom dutifully serving them both and asking them if they want seconds. Her wiping his hands clean with a dish towel after he had gotten them sticky from the syrup jar. Wiping his mouth, just for good measure. She laughs. His dad folds his paper and lays it beside his coffee mug and begins to eat as she takes her place beside him.

A tearful smile spread across Kyle's face as he watched the way his family could have been, should have been. They were so happy together. They would have breakfast, lunch, and dinner together. This kitchen table would bond them. "How's school?" His dad would say. "Are ya making all A's?" "How's that pretty little girl down the street?" "Have you kissed her on the cheek yet?" "How about we go fishing this Saturday?"

"School's great, dad." "She the prettiest girl in the whole school" "No, I haven't kissed her, yet. Soon, hopefully." "Yeah, that would be nice." Kyle would say excitedly.

"Oh, you two." His mother would smile as she took a sip of coffee. Never eating, only watching the two of them. Her two men, interacting, being proud of their father-son bond.

Kyle would hurry up and finish his breakfast. They would tell him to "Slow down. Don't eat so fast." "Finish your milk." He would race down the hallway from the kitchen, grab his books, and head out the screen door, waving bye to his doting mother and father.

Kyle raised his hand and waved to himself, smile fading. He watch the mirrored image behind the screen door as the clouds began to turn dark and a worried look spread across his doppelganger's face. Kyle looked at the kitchen table which was now empty. And back to his second self, who was now gone. He turned and walked outside, across the porch, across the yard.

The day had become dark, stormy…grey clouds covered the sky and blocked out the sun.

Darker and darker, until there was only night.

Melanie stands waiting, then turns and runs into the woods.

A flicker of orange light shines on the well-beaten path. Torches. A bonfire. Flashlights.

Kyle walks slowly. He sees a line of people. Everyone is faced forward, not speaking, not looking, marching solemnly with bowed heads. He walks beside them, following Melanie, looking at each one completely unnoticed.

He recognizes these people. His Sunday school teacher, Mrs. Vonnie Snelling. His third grade elementary teacher, Mrs. Neighbors. That old man that always sits with his Sunday paper in the back of the church, Mr. Clayton. His preacher, Pastor Jim. His mother and his father. No one looks at him as he passes. No one talks to each other.

Kyle comes to the head of the line, to the sign welcoming the lost souls to *The Haunted Woods*.

His friends, Jeremy and Eric, stand on both sides of the entrance handing out tickets to each person that walks through the gate. They didn't talk just gave each person a red piece of paper. Each person that Kyle had passed in the line was now walking past him, taking a ticket from his two friends and proceeding forward.

Kyle waited until everyone in line had gone through. When the last person took their ticket from Jeremy, both boys followed through the gate and closed it behind them, locking Kyle out. They looked at Kyle, then turned and disappeared into the woods.

"Wait!" Kyle yelled. "Melanie is in there!" "My parents are in there!"

The gate was locked. And the trees created a barrier that he could not cross otherwise. He stood listening to the horrible groans and screams as the place began to light up in oranges and reds. Seeing nothing, just the beginning of a flash of light that was beginning to grow stronger. Brighter and brighter, hotter, until it was all consuming, and then a blast of heat.

Kyle woke up soaking wet around his neck. His hair was matted down on his head. His pillow felt soggy and his t-shirt was sticking to his back. He sat up and got out of bed, peeling his t-shirt off and throwing it on the floor. He fumbled for the light. Once he found it, he rummaged through his closet for another t-shirt.

It was okay that he was up. He needed to go the bathroom and pee anyway. That one wasn't that bad. He thought. *Not as bad as the others. In fact, he didn't really know what that one even meant. If it meant anything at all.*

Kyle flicked on the lights to the hallway bathroom, which still kind of stung his eyes. For some reason, Mrs. Harper used high wattage bulbs in the bathroom instead of low watt. Kyle didn't care if she needed them to put on her make-up in the bathroom in her bedroom, but the hallway bathroom was *his* bathroom, a more mellow lighting would have been preferable. Something where he didn't always have to see himself.

Chapter 8

(Saturday Afternoon, Halloween)

Dear whoever gets this,

I feel like things have been bad for awhile, and I don't see them getting any better. In fact, I'm sensing doom. I'm really not sure anymore if I should feel anything. I've gone completely numb. I feel like the reason I am this way is because I've always been surrounded by horrible people that do and say horrible things with no sense of regret, no sense of guilt. I just can't help but think, "What is the point?"

I do feel like I've tried to be happy and that I've tried to console and help others, even people I've never met. But I don't see anyone like me in my social circles. I don't randomly run into people that are kind-hearted, in fact, quite the opposite. Each day, is just another day where I meet selfish, hedonistic people whose only concern in life is to consume and step on those around them.

So, since there is no hope, since there is no future. I don't see the point of trying anymore or being around any longer. I am choosing to end my life and no longer be that burden that people have to deal with. I was never meant for this world. I feel too much and that makes me too soft. I can't be hardened and soulless like all of you people.

Kyle Nathaniel Harper

Kyle sat down his pen and looked blankly at the paper. He reread what he had just written. He felt like these words had pretty much summed up what he was feeling. Even though he said that he was numb and that he didn't feel anything, he lied. It was a big lie, because Kyle felt a lot of things. He felt sorry for his dad and the way his mother had treated him. He felt sorry that he was never that straight-A student and that he would never know what it was like to be a valedictorian. He felt sorry for all those starving children in Africa, who couldn't help that they were born into poverty. Mostly, he felt sorry that he would never be anyone's joy.

The idea of "joy" just seemed incomprehensible, like a word that doesn't translate properly to English from another language. It can't be explained, it just simply has to be felt. But if no one could describe it, the sensation, then how would Kyle ever know when it was real; if it was real.

Was it the same idea as utopia? Kyle sat back in his chair and looked out his window to the world. *Does happiness really exist? You always hear about it. Someone is happy. This person is happy. But what are they saying? Sadness is easy to understand, it's demonstrated, on a daily basis. You can see the melancholy. You can see the suffering. We all understand pain and how severe it can be. We all understand tears and cuts and scrapes and pinches and cramps...the list goes on and on. So what is this "happiness" and "joy" that everyone keeps talking about?*

It's all a myth.

Kyle walked over to his bed and dropped across it. He wondered what it would be like afterwards, after he was dead. He didn't think of everyone else. He just thought about...the silence, the quiet, it being dark, possibly a little chilly and cold. He thought: *maybe death really was hell, the idea of being no more and the torture of wanting to go back and change things, fix them. Maybe hell was a list of memories that we are all stuck to relive. Every time we fell down as a child, or got a whippin' from our parents, or saw some other kid get that toy we always wanted and then break it because they didn't want to play with it anymore.*

What if we were stuck reliving the same nightmares over and over again? The bad nightmares, where there is no one left to save us, it's just down to us and the scary monster that we must all face. Or those sad dreams when someone you love is dead and you can't wake them up. Our memories have got to be our own hell, Kyle thought. *Unless we find a way as human beings to purposely develop amnesia, some people are doomed to suffer a horrible fate because of their past transgressions.*

Kyle also wondered as he lay there curled up if his past transgressions would come back to haunt him. *How much of hell would he have to endure in death? Church teaches us all that we are sinners; will his sins be a light load to bear? Or will he be tortured for the rest of his afterlife?*

Kyle closed his eyes and snuggled up to his teddy bear. A sense of warmth traveled throughout his skin. And without his blanket he fell asleep, but only for a little while, because tonight was the big night, Halloween was finally here. And he promised his father that he would meet him on his journey through *The Haunted Woods*.

"Kyle...Kyle...wake up." A soft voice whispered through the ether.

Chapter 9
(Early Sunday Morning)

Stomp, Stomp, Stomp. Kyle's little baby Nike's stampeded across the concrete sidewalk.

"There he goes! Boy, he's a fast one, ain't he?" Mr. Harper stood at the edge of his truck smiling as he watched his two-year-old son take off.

"I'm gonna getchu!" Mrs. Harper stamped her feet loudly behind Kyle, which made him holler and laugh.

Flop.

Kyle fell face forward and skinned his bare knees on the pavement. A delayed bellow came from the shocked baby as the stinging pain finally registered with his brain. He laid there screaming, trying to catch his breath; waiting for the mother that was so eager on chasing him, to finally pick him up and take care of him.

"Goddamnit Kelly! I told you that you got to be more careful with him. Now his legs are all busted up."

"It's not my fault that he fell! I didn't mean for him to get hurt!"

"Yeah, you never mean to, do you? You fuckin' women, I swear. You can never take care of your damn kids." Mr. Harper snatched Kyle from her arms and carried him inside the bank. The ladies inside stared in awe as the man came through the doors carrying a blood baby.

"Oh my God!" One of the tellers said as she came around the counter to help him.

"Would you mind if I use the restroom to get him cleaned up. His mother was playing a little too rough with him and he got hurt."

***

Kyle stood in the middle of the field. Snow on the ground. Bare trees with white tops stood where *The Haunted Woods* were. The red thickness dripping from his legs painted a picture on the diamonds that bust under his Nike's. He looked away from what once was and began trekking forward, back to town. It was all over. He stumbled and slung the blood sideways. He fell forward onto his side and screamed in agony.

Crunch.

Crunch.

Kyle could hear the ice crystals busting; more and more of them, creating a cacophony of sound. It sounded like a million-man army marching towards him, possibly to march over him. Through the puddles in his eyes, he managed to make out a clear picture of what was headed his way. A heavy figure, covered in fur. Was it a bear? Was he here to finish him off, finish what the demons hadn't?

The furry figure stopped at Kyle's head and kneeled down. Kyle flinched and covered his face.

"Come on, son. Let's get you on your feet."

Kyle recognized that voice.

"I thought you were dead. Everyone's dead...was it all a dream?"

"No. it was real." He helps Kyle to his feet. "It was all real, son."

Kyle jumped back like he was shot as Pastor Jim put his hand on his shoulder. "I'm not your son!" Kyle staggered back as he watched the tidal wave begin to rise in the background. Higher and higher until it was behind the town. "No! Not again!" Kyle ran and hopped back to the woods as each step shot spikes up and down his legs. He screamed in agony with each gallop.

Soon, the town was swallowed. Pastor Jim turned around to see the commotion. He stood there with his arms out, welcoming God's punishment. The gushing waters swallowed around him. Kyle had almost made it to the edge of the woods, when the force of the waves overtook him and slammed his feather-light body into the trees. One by one, the flood uprooted each plant like it was never permanent, only there for ornamental decoration. Kyle's watched as he floated along with the town, along with the people, along with the woods. The heavens came and washed away...it all.

***

Kyle groaned and squinted as he began to regain consciousness. He felt his head, only it wasn't his skin or his hair that he felt. Something rough scratched against the surface of his fingers. He opened his eyes fully to see where he was. He turned his head and looked up at the dripping bag and the blue box that held a monitor inside. Blip, blip, blip. One by one he watched the green mountains as each peak abruptly ended and began and ended and began.

"God, I am crazy!"

Kyle followed the IV cord down to the back of his hand. He lifted his arm the best he could and noticed the symmetry of mummy wrappings around his right wrist…then his left. "It didn't work. I'm still here."

His lungs felt heavy as he tried to sit up more. Kyle placed his hand over his chest to make sure that his heart was actually beating, that this all wasn't just another nightmare. It was weak and he had to hold his hand still for a minute to make sure. "I'm still alive." At first he was happy, then he began to dread what would happen next. Thoughts began to appear: *"What would everyone say?" "Where are his parents?" "Who found him?" "Was any of it true or was it just all imagined?"*

Then, the smart-ass kicked in. "Fuck em!"

Kyle lowered the railing on his bed and swiveled around to put his feet on the floor. His body was weak and his head felt dizzy. He struggled as he put his weight down. He flinched a little at the coldness of the tile on his toes. "Mmmm," and not in a good way. Kyle exhaled heavily holding his stomach as if to keep him from vomiting.

He grabbed the IV stand to steady himself as well as become a rollable cane of sorts. Kyle managed to stand straight up, well, for the most part. Suddenly, he felt this throbbing pain every time he tried to contract his fist. He looked up at the red-soaked underside of his wrist and shook his head. It almost made him nauscious to know that was his blood. He slowly wheeled over to the bathroom door and turned the knob. More pain, Kyle let out a groan and heavy breath. The door opened on its own. Kyle fumbled for the switch.

The bulbs came on slowly and one at a time, as if they were meant to not blind you. They hummed as their coils heated up with electricity. Kyle slinked past the sink and flopped down on to the toilet. *This was going to take some getting use to.* He leaned forward and pulled at his gown to lift it up so he could pee. "Now I have to pee sitting down like a girl, great." It stung at first until his muscles relaxed and allowed for his body to lose more fluid.

"My mouth's dry." Kyle tried to lick his bottom lip, but no wetness manifested itself. He looked at the sink. No cup manifested itself either. He looked down between his legs, still peeing. He let out a deep sigh, "as always." After a few seconds, it stopped. He shook himself free and stood up with a grunt. He reached over and pushed the leaver down with his knuckles.

Kyle stumbled over to the sink and pulled the silver lever. The water came out with force, splashing outward from the bottom of the sink. Kyle just stared at the violence of it all. The force, the cold, the red…Kyle looked at his left wrist, and didn't realize that he must have cut it deeper than his right. There was blood on his gown. He looked in the mirror and saw blood on his face, trickling down from the bandage on his head.

Steam began to rise from the sink. Kyle smeared red lines across the mirror as he tried to see through the blur. The bathroom door slammed behind him as Junior put his hand over his mouth. Kyle began to fight and scream, but Junior had him in a vice grip that he couldn't get out of. Kyle kicked as he picked him up from behind. He saw the blood bandages on his knees. He kicked and pushed until the bathroom door came open.

Kyle swung his arm down as hard as he could and hit Junior in the groin. Kyle was immediately dropped to the floor. "Help me!" Kyle slid as he was getting up to run and fell back down with the IV stand falling over top of him. "Somebody help me! Please!" He cried and screamed at the same time.

Two orderlies and Kyle's mother ran into the room. One

orderly grabbed Kyle's shoulders, while the other tried to grab his feet but slipped on the puddle of blood in the floor. "I thought he was strapped down!" Kyle's mother said to the men. Kyle looked at the straps hanging on the side of the bed. "No! You bitch! I'm not crazy, he's in there! Somebody help me, he's in there!" They wrestled Kyle into the bed. "Hold him down!" The orderly motioned to Kyle's mother.

"Why are you doing this to me? He's in there! Where's dad? Daddy!" Kyle flinched as the big black guy shoved a needle in his arm. "Ow. Ow."

"There." The big man said. "He ain't going no where for a while."

"I want my dad." Kyle's head rolled back and forth across the pillow. "Where's daddy?"

The orderly looked at Kyle's mother and then stepped back. Mrs. Harper leaned up closer. "Kyle, your father passed away when you were four. Don't you remember?" Kyle stared at her in fear, then looked past her to the bathroom and Junior standing in the doorway, slowly fading backwards into the darkness. Her voice began to trail off as Kyle began to fade as well. "He died in a boating accident on the river. You remember, don't you?"

"No, daddy was here. *The Haunted Woods.* Pastor Jim told me he was my real father. Daddy married you to save your name…"

"Who told you that?!" Mrs. Harper began to shake Kyle. "No one knows that! Who told you that?! It's a lie!

The orderlies grabbed her as she began choking Kyle. "Mrs. Harper! Mrs. Harper! Control yourself! Security!" They dragged her out of the room.

"You ungrateful brat! I gave up everything for you!" Mrs. Harper screamed as they dragged her down the hallway.

"You bitch." Kyle shook his head and looked at Junior in

the bathroom. He stood for a while motionless in the dark, then he removed his mask.

Kyle squinted through the tears that had welled up in his eyes. Suddenly, everything came into focus.

"Daddy?"

Chapter 10
(Saturday Night, Halloween)

"I'm awake." Kyle rubbed his eyes. "I'm awake." He had knocked Polo Bear onto the floor. *Must have been another violent sleep,* he thought. Kyle stretched an popped his knee. "Man, that was loud." He turned and put his feet on the floor and just sat there rocking back and forth for a moment. "Uh, time to get up and motorvate." His body rose up, still head down, and solemnly marched to the bathroom. "Time to pee again, as always." Nothing came out this time. "Okay, maybe not." Kyle flushed the toilet anyway and turned the light on as he walked out to escape the blinding pain.

"Should I wear a costume tonight?" He opened his closet. "I have jeans and a black button-down Ralph Lauren or I have a green Polo polo...polo, polo, polo. Everything is a polo by Polo. There's a mask but no real costume. I'll wear normal clothes. Don't want to be confused with the others." Kyle threw a random button-down and a pair of jeans on his bed. "Okay, now I have to pee."

Kyle walked back to the bathroom. This time, the light didn't sting as bad since his eyes had time to adjust. He started to feel weak. "I need to sit." Kyle pulled down his boxer briefs and sat on the commode. "I'm dreading this. It's stupid anyways." Kyle relaxed and took a deep breath, finally he could feel the pressure lessen and a steady stream released itself from his body. After what seemed to Kyle like an eternity, "Okay, you can stop now. God, I can't believe I'm still going." He took another deep breath and began tapping his foot. "Any day now…" Kyle sat and waited. "Okay. Finally." The stream lost its force but was still making and effort. "Oh come on." Kyle strained and then shook, strained and then shook. "Nope, there's still more. Good God." Drip, Drip, Drip. Kyle shook one more time. "I think we're empty now. No more fluids."

Kyle pulled his boxer briefs back up. "Now we can go." He looked in the mirror and saw how pale he looked. His face seemed like it had sunken from dehydration. Kyle grabbed two handfuls of water from the faucet and splashed it on his face, but it didn't seem to help. The water just rolled right off. He rubbed his face vigorously with a towel and put it back on the hanger. "I need to go before I'm late."

The shirt and pants he picked out seemed plain enough. No need to stand out when being hunted by axe murderers. He wondered who would be in the woods, besides his dad's friends. How many church-goers would be meeting him along the way? He always hated this anticipation right before any encounter with large crowds. It was always the same no matter what; a sense of death.

Kyle threw his gym bag into the truck and hopped up in the cab. "This ought to be interesting." He started the truck and pulled out onto the highway. No sign of *The Haunted Woods* yet. No lights. No Vegas signs promoting a headlining event. Nothing, just darkness.

Kyle drove past the city limits. "It's kinda sad that what separates us from going somewhere is this, like the obstacle or gauntlet that we have to overcome." After the bend in the road, the outline of *The Haunted Woods* became clear. There seemed to be a blue glow around it, showcasing it. There was the sign saying "turn here, come here" or "stay away, go away. Run Kyle." No such luck. He had to go.

Hell approached as he drove past the last house on the right. All that was separating him was a small field and a line of cars and trucks. Kyle found an empty spot where his truck would fit. "Perfect." Kyle squeezed it in slowly and shut off the engine.

It sounded like he was parked next to the railroad tracks. Loud changing, buzzing, screaming, and music. It sounded like someone had opened the door to hell to let out the noise. *We danced on the ground above an unholy spot. If only it would just cave in. How far down would we fall before hitting bottom?* Kyle sat staring out the windshield. *Nothing or no one should ever come here and yet here we are.* The strobe lights began flickering, creating white blotches over his pupils. "It's time."

Kyle grabbed his bag and got out of the truck. "They're already waiting in line. Standing in purgatory, waiting on hell." Kyle looked at each one of them as he walked by. Most didn't pay him any attention: conversating, anxiously awaiting what's to come, little kids holding onto their parents for dear life saying, "I don't want to go. I want to go home," parents not listening, couples hugging—damn near making out. A long line of sinners just waiting to be served hell's justice.

The gravel road people were lined up on was kept open so trucks could pass through, if not ambulances or police cars. The fire chief was always on hand as well as the sheriff. Dad didn't like either. Of course, no on would ever know it. He was pretty good about hiding.

"You ready for this, hun?" Kyle recognized the voice behind the green face and long nose.

"I always knew you were a witch."

"Not a real one like you."

"Aww, you say the sweetest things. Where's dad?"

"He's here." Mable grabbed an open book slammed it on the table in front of him. "You have to sign your name in his book if you want to go in."

"I don't have a pen."

"No need." Mable grabbed his wrist and jabbed it with a pin.

"Ow." Kyle dropped his bag to jerk his wrist back.

"You'll be fine now." Mable smeared his blood across the page and it disappeared, so did the cut on his wrist. The gate began to open. "Go on." Mable nodded with her head. Kyle looked at her confused and mesmerized at the same time.

He picked up his bag and walked through the entrance. A sign was nailed to a tree with the words "TOO LATE" etched in black soot. Kyle knew everyone was hiding. He just didn't know where. The place looked empty. He turned around to see if he could perhaps get a look at the lost souls outside. They looked orange and blurry. It almost hurt to look at them. Kyle turned his attention back to the task at hand. "Gotta find dad." He began to walk until he came to a gypsy tent with a tarot reader inside.

"Can I help you on your journey child?"

"Have you seen him?"

"From time to time." He was being cryptic, so Kyle decided to play along.

"Will I see him this night?"

"You will always see him child. In your dreams, when your head begins to ache. Though, he is not the one you search for."

"He's not?"

"You seek your father and he is not here."

"That's who I was talking about."

"The man you speak of is not your father."

"Then who is he?"

"A Daemon. A Daemon of the worst kind."

"Why would I seek a Daemon?"

"You are his child."

"But you just said he wasn't my father!" Kyle became frustrated. "Okay stop the bullshit, where's my dad?"

"You are in grave danger of becoming like him."

"I'm out of here." Kyle got up and the old man grabbed his wrist.

"There is a girl who is lost."

Kyle stood still for a moment. "She dumped me."

The old sage waved his hand over his crystal ball. "She's dead, but her spirit is trapped along the highway."

"Okay, I'm gonna go now."

"You must find her and set her ghost free. It is your only redemption."

"Happy Halloween." Kyle pulled out his hockey mask from his bag and pushed through the hanging beads. "Fuckin' weirdo." Kyle knelt down over his bag and pulled out a hand sickle. "Never leave home without it." He tossed the bag over his shoulder and began to walk down the dirt path.

RRmrmrmrmrmrmrmrmrrmrmr Rrmmrmrmrmrmmmrmrmrmr!

Kyle tapped his masked with his sickle at Junior and pretended to not be scared as he kept walking. He noticed Junior's head tilt in an awkward curious dog sort of way. He didn't know if it would make Junior angry that he wasn't scared or if he would simply shrug it off and go pester someone else. So far, no retaliation. *Whew!*

For some reason, Junior was the only one that really scared him. He guessed it was the unsettling noise of the chainsaw and how loud it was. It was earsplitting. *God, can't people kill others in silence? It would be non-climactic yes, but at least a little more pleasant.*

Kyle jumped.

"Jesus Christ!" Kyle grabbed his chest. "Sorry Jesus, no pun intended."

"How did you know it was me?" Jason Deproe pulled up his hockey mask.

"Because your hair's like Jesus. Plus, I knew that you were wearing the same mask as me."

"Aw, you cheated." He put his mask back on.

"Have you seen dad around here." It sounded so loud when he talked behind the mask.

"I'm suppose to be your guide."

"Are we suppose to lock arms or something?"

Jesus pulled out his arm sickle.

"No way." Kyle raised his sickle as well .

"Too fuckin' weird."

"Tell me about it dude. Well, come on Jesus, lead me through hell."

"That's my job." He clinked his sickle against Kyle's.

Despite the obvious humor in the situation, Kyle still kept wondering why everyone has been acting so damn odd here lately, more than usual. It unnerved him what that old man said. *What girl was he talking about?*

He followed Jesus for as long as he could until he told him to stop. "I gotta take a piss. Hold up."

"I can't wait. I have to keep going."

"Well go on. I'll catch up." Kyle walked around to the other side of the nearest tree. *Well at least now I won't pee in my pants.* Kyle looked around him as he was relieving himself to see if anyone was coming. No one. Jesus had already left him behind. Still going. "Come on. Don't do this now?"

Grunt.

Kyle's mask smashed into the tree. He toppled over in a daze. "What the fuck man?!" He stumbled to his feet. His mask seemed fine, but his pants were unzipped and his dick was still out. He turned to face his attacker and began peeing again. Kyle and Junior looked down to see the front of Junior's overalls covered in piss.

"GRrrrrrr!"

Kyle stopped peeing and put his dick back in his underwear and zipped up his pants. "Sorry." He said trying not to laugh. *Oh, this motherfucker's going to kill me.* Kyle walked around the tree as Junior stared at him menacingly.

Rmrmrmrmrmrmrrmrm Rmrmrmrmrmrmrmmrmr.

"Oh Shit!" Kyle took off running. "Stupid Redneck fuck's gonna cut my dick off!" Kyle fell again. This time, he left his bag and just kept his sickle. *Come on, you fucker, you wanna go?* Kyle ran for as long as he could until Junior caught up to him. He rubbed the chainsaw up Kyle's forearm causing him to drop his sickle. Kyle screamed and huddle down clenching his wrist, causing Junior to fly over him.

"That's what you get dumbass!"

Tears blurred his eyes and then he noticed that the chainsaw had stopped. Kyle wiped his eyes, smearing blood across his cheek. Junior had landed on top of his weapon of choice. "Oh God." Kyle got up and walked over to 300 pound mass on the ground. Kyle nudged him with his foot. No movement. "Oh

God!" Kyle moved around his body to take a closer look at what actually happened. The blade was stuck in his head from the top of his ear down to the base of his neck. "Oh God!!"

Kyle reluctantly grabbed the blade and Junior's head and tried to separate them. His skin pulled and more blood poured out. Kyle began to hyperventilate and backed away.

"It wasn't your fault." Mr. Harper came up behind him.

"Yes it was. I should have never let you talk me into coming here."

"Everyone comes here. It's tradition."

"No. This is stupid." Kyle began to sob. "You're not my father, are you?"

"What? Who told you that?"

"Is it true?" Kyle got up and walked further down the path leaving his mask on the ground. He could hear semi's driving down the highway. He was almost out of the woods.

"He doesn't know what's true and what's not anymore, hun."

"I know he loves you. My mom's a whore. And I'm the bastard son of a preacher."

"So you got it all figured out, do you?" Mable was no longer wearing her witch's costume. Now she was dressed normally.

"Yep."

"Mr. Harper didn't love me. He raped me."

Kyle looked at her as she led him to the highway.

"Right here is where it happened. I was hitchhiking into town. He stopped to give me a ride or so I thought." She stopped moving. "This is where he stopped the car. He pulled me out and dragged me over here, into the woods, where we're standing." Kyle looked down at the ground and then back up at Mable. "He told me not to scream or he would kill me. He held a knife to my throat until he was finished. When he was finished, he was finished with me. He slid the knife across my throat and left me here, bleeding, like you are now." She grabbed his wrist with both hands. "It will be alright." She lifted her hands away and all the blood and torn skin was gone.

"So what am I suppose to do now."

"Live…as best as you can, knowing now what you know."

"Will I ever see you again?"

"I hope not hun. It means that neither of us ever left and you shouldn't be here anymore." Mable came closer to Kyle and hugged him.

"Bye Mable." Kyle noticed that she got younger until she turned into Melanie. Kyle began to cry again. "No. He didn't do this to you." Melanie nodded.

"Why?"

"You had to come to terms with it on your own. People are never what they seem."

"Is everyone dead?"

"Everyone here, yes."

"Am I dead too?"

"Only if you want to be." Melanie began walking up to the highway. "You can stay here Kyle Harper, in these woods, in this doorway to hell, or you can choose to go back to where you came. The choice is always yours." Melanie stuck out her thumb. She was now holding the bag that Kyle had been carrying. A red convertible Mustang stopped in the middle of the road.

"Bye Melanie." Kyle said to himself as the car drove away. He crossed the highway to an empty lot. He was the only one left or maybe he was the only one there to begin with. He started his truck. Buddy Holly was on the radio.

"Love like yours will surely come my way."

Kyle turned it up and pulled out onto the highway.

Epilogue

So today I'm going back to Waterville for the first time since I graduated high school. I forgot how scenic the drive was down here in late October. The corn fields have all been picked and the cotton fields look like fluffy white snow. I love to drive in a country or vineyard setting. There are usually no cars, no people, just me and the road. It's freeing in a way. I usually put the top down, strap my seatbelt on, turn the radio up loud, and off I go. I listen to the sound of the wind over the music as it clears my head. It's an ethereal experience. It's probably the closest thing I'll ever get to flying.

Somehow, today I don't feel like flying though. I didn't even put the top down. I didn't turn the radio on. I'm just sitting here, my eyes glued to the highway, not noticing the cars passing by. The air sounds different outside my windows, like the thickness of a strong undercurrent pushing me in the direction it wants me to go. The tidal wave has once again swallowed me and now I'm here, waiting to drown.

I forgot that everyone in these small towns wave to one

another as they pass each other on the road. It's a friendly oddness because it leaves people vulnerable. While I'm recognizing the familiarity of death, it doesn't take long for me to pass through Waterville. I didn't go through town; I went down the highway outside of town. We used to always joke that if you blinked, you would pass our town without even knowing it. To this day, I still blink. I blink a couple times. It's still there, unfortunately.

I can see the outline of *The Haunted Woods* as I reach the edge of the first field. They appear smaller than what I remember. They must have cut a lot of it down. They used to be way back, three or four times farther than what it is now.

My car's tires become quieter on the highway, almost like a whisper. I slowly press my brakes as I approach. I slow down and watch in awe of how tall the trees still are and even with the overall mass shortened from what it used to be, I still can't see straight through. All these strategically placed trees.

I turn down the gravel road beside the woods. Even this road, seems to be freshly grated and taken care of. The ditches along the road have been mowed. The corn field has been plowed. Every detail looks very manicured.

I stop the car and roll down the window half-way as I pull up to a sign that says "Entrance." I look around, from one end of the woods to the next. I look down the dirt road and then look down the highway. No cars, no people. I look back at the sign. Underneath *"Entrance"* reads *"The Haunted Woods,"* under that, *"The Scariest Place On Earth!"*

I stare vacantly at the sign and then get out of my car. I walk around to the trunk and click the button on my keychain for it to open. I grab my hand saw and march straight over to the sign.

As I begin to slide the blade across the timber, I can't help but feel a rage swelling up inside of me, like my heart is going to explode out of my chest. *It's starting again...It's starting again.* I make it through one leg and then start on the next. Quickly the sign falls back onto the grass. I turn and march back to my trunk, throw the saw in, and slam the lid.

I look defiantly at the monstrosity standing before me as tears stream down my face. Years of my life are gone because of this place. My family. My friends. Everything taken away. And for what? Good Halloween fun? It was never in good fun.

I get back in my car and squeeze the steering wheel as my body convulses. I rock back and forth rubbing my chest and taking deep breaths. "Just breathe, Kyle." It's not helping. I fling open the console. "Where are my pills?" I fumble through the gas receipts, the checkbook, the pens, stupid matchbooks, and at the very bottom, there's a bottle. As force of habit, I look at the label first, always. I read to make sure. My temples hurt so bad I can hardly focus enough to read the label. *Lithium. Take as directed.* I open the bottle. Empty.

I throw the bottle in the passenger-side floorboard and open the door to my car. "I just need some air." I step out of the car and begin fanning myself as I pace back and forth. I kneel down beside my back tire. "Just stop!" I sob as I pound my head with my fists. "It isn't real! It isn't real!" I know it's a lie, but I tell myself that anyways because maybe if I say it out loud, it will make it a reality.

"I can't keep doing this." I struggle to cough and almost dry-heave. I look up from the road to the ditch, from the ditch to the woods. I breathe. I stand up as I hear an eighteen-wheeler coming down the highway. I wipe my eyes and get back in my car. I start the engine and pull up to the entrance. I immediately throw the car in reverse and back out. I sling rocks and dirt behind me as I hit the gas to go forward. I see the eighteen-wheeler coming. He sees me coming to. He sees me pick up speed. If I time it just right, I'll be right in front of him when he hits me.

He honks his horn and veers to the left. I slow down to a stop. *Dammit!* I sit there staring, for what seems like forever. I don't even know what I'm looking at or what to think. *This could have all been over, and yet...It's starting again.* I begin rocking back and forth...

I don't even notice when a man in a leather mask slams his chainsaw into my window.

Commentary

Obviously, this story is an homage to so many great stories of the past like "Our Town" "Turn of the Screw" "Young Goodman Brown" "The Scarlet Letter" which are all perfect examples of how people will show their true selves when they believe that no one is watching; "no one" including God. The woods outside of town serve as a hiding place, a recess for the mind, and an indulgence in a hedonistic way of life. If we pose the town against the woods, we see that the townsfolk of Waterville, MO, have a separation from their ideal self and their real self—their Christ-like self and their human self.

By using the Freudian approach of the Id vs. the Superego, the reading audience can further understand how temptation can lure even the most renowned Christian into a life of debauchery. While there is a modernization and modification of the circumstances in this story, the parallel flaws of humanity inside of people remain the same.

Lightning Source UK Ltd.
Milton Keynes UK
UKOW041850270912

199760UK00001B/123/P